Love Hazard

Also From Rachel Van Dyken

Mafia Royals
Royal Bully
Ruthless Princess
Scandalous Prince
Destructive King
Fallen Royal
Broken Crown

Liars, Inc.
Dirty Exes
Dangerous Exes

Covet Series
Stealing Her
Finding Him

Bro Code Series
Co-Ed
Seducing Mrs. Robinson
Avoiding Temptation
The Set-Up

Elite Bratva Brotherhood
Debase

The Players Game Series
Fraternize
Infraction
MVP

The Consequence Series
The Consequence of Loving Colton
The Consequence of Revenge
The Consequence of Seduction
The Consequence of Rejection

The Wingmen Inc. Series
The Matchmaker's Playbook
The Matchmaker's Replacement

Curious Liaisons Series
Cheater
Cheater's Regret

The Bet Series
The Bet
The Wager
The Dare

The Ruin Series
Ruin
Toxic
Fearless
Shame

The Eagle Elite Series
Elite
Elect
Enamor
Entice
Elicit
Bang Bang
Enforce
Ember
Elude
Empire
Enrage
Eulogy
Envy

The Seaside Series
Tear
Pull
Shatter
Forever
Fall
Eternal
Strung
Capture

The Renwick House Series
The Ugly Duckling Debutante
The Seduction of Sebastian St. James

An Unlikely Alliance
The Redemption of Lord Rawlings
The Devil Duke Takes a Bride

The London Fairy Tales Series
Upon a Midnight Dream
Whispered Music
The Wolf's Pursuit
When Ash Falls

The Seasons of Paleo Series
Savage Winter
Feral Spring

The Wallflower Series (with Leah Sanders)
Waltzing with the Wallflower
Beguiling Bridget
Taming Wilde

The Dark Ones Saga
The Dark Ones
Untouchable Darkness
Dark Surrender
Darkest Temptation
Darkest Sinner

Stand-Alones
Mafia Casanova (with M Robinson)
Hurt: A Collection (with Kristin Vayden and Elyse Faber)
Rip
Compromising Kessen
Every Girl Does It
The Parting Gift (with Leah Sanders)
Divine Uprising
A Crown for Christmas

Love Hazard

By Rachel Van Dyken

1001 DARK NIGHTS
PRESS

Love Hazard
By Rachel Van Dyken
Copyright 2024
ISBN: 979-8-88542-086-0

Published by 1001 Dark Nights Press, an imprint of Evil Eye Concepts, Incorporated

All rights reserved. No part of this book may be reproduced, scanned, or distributed in any printed or electronic form without permission. Please do not participate in or encourage piracy of copyrighted materials in violation of the author's rights.

This is a work of fiction. Names, places, characters and incidents are the product of the author's imagination and are fictitious. Any resemblance to actual persons, living or dead, events or establishments is solely coincidental.

Sign up for the 1001 Dark Nights Newsletter
and be entered to win a Tiffany Key necklace.

There's a contest every month!

Go to www.1001DarkNights.com to subscribe.

**As a bonus, all subscribers can download
FIVE FREE exclusive books!**

One Thousand and One Dark Nights

Once upon a time, in the future…

I was a student fascinated with stories and learning. I studied philosophy, poetry, history, the occult, and the art and science of love and magic. I had a vast library at my father's home and collected thousands of volumes of fantastic tales.

I learned all about ancient races and bygone times. About myths and legends and dreams of all people through the millennium. And the more I read the stronger my imagination grew until I discovered that I was able to travel into the stories... to actually become part of them.

I wish I could say that I listened to my teacher and respected my gift, as I ought to have. If I had, I would not be telling you this tale now. But I was foolhardy and confused, showing off with bravery.

One afternoon, curious about the myth of the Arabian Nights, I traveled back to ancient Persia to see for myself if it was true that every day Shahryar (Persian: شهریار, "king") married a new virgin, and then sent yesterday's wife to be beheaded. It was written and I had read that by the time he met Scheherazade, the vizier's daughter, he'd killed one thousand women.

Something went wrong with my efforts. I arrived in the midst of the story and somehow exchanged places with Scheherazade – a phenomena that had never occurred before and that still to this day, I cannot explain.

Now I am trapped in that ancient past. I have taken on Scheherazade's life and the only way I can protect myself and stay alive is to do what she did to protect herself and stay alive.

Every night the King calls for me and listens as I spin tales. And when the evening ends and dawn breaks, I stop at a point that leaves him breathless and yearning for more. And so the King spares my life for one more day, so that he might hear the rest of my dark tale.

As soon as I finish a story... I begin a new one... like the one that you, dear reader, have before you now.

Prologue

"If it ends with sushi, it starts with sushi."—August Wellington

Hazel

Summer 2016

I peered around my favorite tree, smack-dab in the middle of our front yard. We'd inherited the house from my great-grandma Nadine. She had been a force to be reckoned with when she was alive and told my dad—her eldest grandson—that she'd had a premonition I would need my own place of solace. Somewhere to read and hide. She then told him she'd disown him if he didn't build a little rope ladder leading to the top.

He tried to call her bluff.

It didn't work.

She stood her ground, which was almost always followed by her tapping a red or leopard-print heel until he gave in—which he always did.

Now that I was seventeen, he wanted me to help out with the family businesses during the summer, but how many chores could a person do?

Each of our vineyards, the farm, and even corporate, had an insane number of staff members, and I still had to wake up at seven to help my mom with the garden. It was midsummer. I was supposed to have some semblance of freedom before my senior year.

The midafternoon was hot, and I just wanted a break. Dad always said my life wasn't stressful, but he knew nothing about the drama in high school, especially living with the awkward, gangly body I still hadn't grown into: weird, stringy blond hair that refused to grow past my boobs; and oh, boobs that *also* refused to grow.

If I weren't so tall, I'd get shoved into lockers. Apparently, my mom had been popular. So had my dad and even my uncle. But the universe failed to send those genes down. It was like everything stopped with them.

Ugh. Even my great-grandma had been cool.

Before she started deteriorating, we'd all assumed she would just move back into the house and allow us to take care of her. Instead, we found her missing daily, heels gone, lipstick snatched, and designer purse off the hook.

My dad said she'd moved back in to haunt him, even while she was still alive. Then again, she was the matriarch of the family and had set up the great Pacific Northwest Titus empire in a way that was unmatched—unless you brought up the name Wellington. One of Great-Grandma Nadine's past lovers. I swore she both blushed and stomped out of the room every time you did.

It was a story we all assumed she'd never tell. We were right. But oddly, she went to Arizona a lot for business, even when she was supposed to be retired.

Weird.

I shook the errant thought from my head; she wouldn't mind if I took a short break. I grabbed my copy of *Pride and Prejudice*—cliche, I know—scurried up the rope ladder into the giant oak and lay down in my favorite spot right where the large leaves blocked the sun. My legs dangled on either side of the branch. The trunk was itchy, even against my white tank, and my jean shorts would probably be indecent if I wore them at school. Oh, good, I was getting even taller.

I groaned, pulled my hair into a ponytail, and got back to my book, only to hear a throat clearing at the base of the tree.

I knew that sound.

It was a trigger.

One I had nightmares about. "No."

"Hazel." His voice was deep and raspy. "You know your dad's going to be pissed if he finds you shirking your responsibilities up there. We all have crosses to bear."

I slammed my book shut and looked down.

The person with the inability to *not* clear his throat in my presence, also known as August Wellington III, stood grinning up at me. He was one of our rich neighbors—a class above me, just graduated, and a total waste of space.

He'd rather fix motorcycles than join the family business, which was some weird art empire that stretched from the East Coast to the West, with around seven locations.

Then again, I couldn't imagine him being an art dealer when he couldn't even shower.

"Shirking. Is it a big-word day?"

He leaned his muscular body against the tree. I hated that we almost matched with his ripped jeans and tight, dirty white tank top. He was so annoying.

"Just because I don't want to go to college doesn't mean I'm stupid," he argued, running a hand through his sandy-brown hair.

I rolled my eyes and went back to my book. "Your hand's greasy, and now your hair looks even worse than it did before. Actually, maybe it's an improvement since it takes the attention away from your nose. Shouldn't you be worrying about yourself? You're a hot mess and probably couldn't get into college unless your dad bribed the board."

He laughed. I hated his laugh. It was always mocking as if what I said was funny—but only to him. It was so stupid. "You mean how your dad bribed me so I'd be your friend?"

I lifted the book into the air, ready to chuck it at him. "Take it back."

"It's true, though." He smiled. I hated how good-looking he was, even with grease all over his face. His high cheekbones and green eyes should be a crime against humanity. "Remember? When you were fourteen and getting bullied, and he gave me money to protect you? Damn, I was like the mafia. Getting paid for protection and to make sure you were safe."

Tears welled in my eyes. "It's just a rumor."

"Rumor?" He leaned against the tree until he was close enough to my leg to tug it. "I'm shocked you don't still wear Keds. Then again, you *are* still growing. Maybe future you has a serious responsibility. Not all heroes wear capes. Maybe instead of college, your thing is to find the magic bean to make people tall."

"Hilarious. And we all know your girlfriend started that rumor."

"Not a rumor. Truth." He leaned in. "Which means it's my responsibility to tell your dad right now that you've taken a time out because the heat is just so intense. Poor spoiled little princess."

"Poor spoiled prince!" I yelled back at him, flailing my arms, only to slip and fall.

He broke my fall with his head, but my arm hit the ground at a weird angle. The crack was so loud that I shook with it.

Tears burned the backs of my eyes. "Leave me alone, August."

"But your arm…" He reached for me, but I jerked away in pain. "I think it's broken. I heard a crack."

"Oh. Well, maybe my dad will give you more money to make it feel better," I yelled as tears started to truly fall down my cheeks.

I hated him.

I hated him so much. He always made everything worse. Made me feel worse. He teased and teased and teased.

Just like everyone else.

What if my dad really did pay him to be my friend?

My stomach sank. Knowing that I had to go into senior year while facing the rumors that he and his girlfriend spread—that I was so pathetic and friendless that my rich dad had to pay the boy next door—was worse than the physical throbbing in my left arm.

"Is it?" I asked in a choked whisper. "Is it actually true? Did he pay you?"

August's eyes locked on mine, and he slowly nodded. "But not in the way you think—"

"I never want to see you again." I sounded calm, but I was shaking from both emotional and physical pain. "Go away."

"Hazel, I was just teasing earlier. I would—"

"Leave me alone," I spat. "Now."

The loudness brought both my mom and dad out.

"Hazel…" August leaned down to touch me, but I kicked at him, jarring my arm more as I rolled over in pain. "Stay still."

"Stay gone," I whispered. "You're a hazard to my health."

"But—"

"GO AWAY!" I screamed.

So, he did.

And I wouldn't see him again for six years.

Chapter One

"Bear spray should be used with all caution unless it's dark, then you just spray until the screaming stops. After all, bears get intimidated by noise, right?"—Hazel Titus

August

Present Day

There were a lot of cars parked in the Titus's driveway, an obscene number, which just seemed strange, even for them. They hosted events during the holidays, but it was June, and in all the years I'd lived in our house helping take care of my mom while my dad traveled for business, I'd never once seen an event that big.

"Hmmmm." I kept sipping my coffee and staring out the window.

"Stalking?" My mom came up behind me. "Again?"

"Yes, because only the good stalkers are careful to watch in plain sight. Throws the victims off. I saw it on *Dateline* once. I would have graduated at the top of my class in stalker school. Ah, damn it. Missed opportunities."

She patted me softly on the shoulder. It was a weak pat, just like it always was since her stroke four years ago—right when I was supposed to be going to college after taking a year off. Right when my life was supposed to begin...

Not that I hated my life, I was just a bit bored. But I felt like I couldn't complain because at least I didn't have to give up working altogether like my mom did. She'd started our companies. Now? She could read, go for some walks, nap, and maybe binge-watch *Yellowstone*. Her heart was weak, the left side of her face was still slack, and she tired easily—even with only being in her late fifties.

I sighed and looked away. "Mom, let me grab you a blanket." I reached for her favorite quilt and was ready to settle her back onto the couch when I heard the fireworks.

I turned around and looked out the window.

Mom grabbed my arm and held onto it. "They must be celebrating something huge."

"Yeah." I patted her hand and pulled her close. "Must be incredible."

I kept in the small amount of jealousy I had that Hazel could live her life while I was stuck with mine. I was happy, and yes, I would love my mom until the very end, but it didn't make it any easier when I saw a party next door and a spoiled brat who had no idea how nice she had it.

I think I'd forever call it a flicker in the matrix. Something that made you pause.

A flicker—and more flickers—of her blond hair as she hugged her dad like she'd just cured cancer or something.

Her smile was huge.

She was wearing black, though.

And then I noticed that everyone was.

Frowning, I dropped my mom's hand. "Be right back."

She sat in her chair and nodded as if she knew my thoughts better than I did. I walked outside and next door. Right into that party.

Amidst the loudness and laughter, I realized too late...

It wasn't a party.

It was a funeral.

Chapter Two

"Lipstick does not heal head trauma."—*August Wellington*

Hazel

"Make it bright," Great-Grandma said. I held her hand, and she wore the hat we'd gotten her as a gag gift: You Need Jesus.

At the time, we'd laughed. I was too young to understand what the moment meant. And *in* that moment, I'd collected all the memories of her smell, the way she patted my hand, and how her laughter always made everyone around her smile.

I never truly imagined a world where she didn't exist. And then, suddenly, she was gone, and I was holding her hat and setting it on a cold, hard grave, unable to see the inscriptions because of the tears in my eyes. Most people left flowers, but I felt like, even in Heaven, Great-Grandma would laugh if she saw the black and white hat with its sparkles. I couldn't bear to take it back with me and prayed it would just stay by her side or get taken by the wind.

My dad ended up buying a new one for me as a reminder of the strong woman who'd come before me, and I always kept in the tears that I'd only had a few years with her until she was gone.

When I finally received my diploma and came home, I'd made a decision. I didn't want a normal graduation party; I wanted to celebrate her life and make it something we did every summer.

Remember her, celebrate, wear crazy hats, and honor her

memory—especially for my cousins and my younger brother, who'd only had her for three years.

"You doing good?" My dad walked up to me and kissed my head, then pulled me into his arms. He always smelled like fresh water and cloves. It was a weird combination, but it *was* comforting. He also always gave the best hugs. He said he'd learned from the best, so that made sense. Great-Grandma was freakishly strong, even into her nineties.

I didn't trust my voice, so I just sank against him. "She always wanted me to get my degree in something brilliant, and I literally changed my major three times and ended up with social sciences after failing statistics. So, really, the fact that I even got my degree is a win." I smiled through the stupid tears falling down my cheeks.

She'd been my best friend.

My hero.

And now, she was gone.

"She didn't even graduate college." Dad rubbed my back, his palm warm against my too-tight, strappy sundress as his fingers moved back and forth, back and forth. "And if she *did* finish college, I imagine her climbing every tree on campus, security chasing her down with flashlights and having a food fight in the cafeteria after having an argument with her psych professor over his love of bad poetry."

I looked up at him. He sported long, brown hair and had crinkles at the corners of his eyes that just made him more handsome. "That was literally so detailed I'm alarmed."

"Well, she was a detailed woman. Now, let's go celebrate her life and your accomplishments after graduating Portland State."

I groaned and made a face. "Do we have to? You know I'd prefer a book, the tree house that you and Mom helped build, and maybe one of your famous lime margaritas."

"The margarita and tree house I can do. The book I can't, because you'll end up stuck in the corner of the treehouse for hours and we do have a lot of people here to honor her and you. So, let's just go back in, say all your greetings, and then I'll make up an excuse for you to escape."

I turned and threw my arms around him. "Aw, best dad ever."

"Grandma would have done the same." He winked. "But seriously, your mom's going to kill us if we don't head back into the party. What's with you and this tree, anyway?"

It was tall, beautiful, the perfect reading spot, and important to me with its bright green leaves and long branches that stretched into the sky.

I used to climb when I wanted to mentally send hate notes to August after he'd made fun of me, and then it just became my thing. I'd escape to it, staring at the house next door and hating that I was wondering what he was doing after high school every time I came home on a break. Until I found out that his life hadn't turned out the way he'd expected either.

I'd lost my great-grandma.

He was losing his mom.

He didn't get to go to school, while I did.

And yeah, life just didn't turn out the way I expected it to. Now, I was stuck wondering what would have happened if we had actually become friends. I'd always had a crush on him, at least until the stupid repeat offender kept making me feel bad about myself. Now, I was left feeling bad for him for no reason. We hadn't talked in years.

But still.

I shook my head at my dad. "Nothing, I just like the tree. It's soothing."

"Soothing." He nodded. "All right. Well, I'm going to head back in. You have five minutes before your mom comes to hunt you down, or your little brother comes and farts in front of you just to make sure you're still alive."

Chapter Three

"There was a reason Cinderella had slippers—weaponry."—Hazel Titus

August

She was by the tree.

"Be right back," I told Mom, who had already fallen asleep on the chair and was tucked in with her blanket.

Her name fell off the tip of my tongue. "Hazel."

I don't know how she heard it the minute I was out my door, but she blinked her eyes open and looked up at me, their blue color so damn pretty. Her hair was longer, and she'd matured, that was for sure, but she'd always been innocent and beautiful—despite the mouth her great-grandma left her with.

I had no clue why girls with fuller top lips than the bottom ones seemed to always have the final word, but Hazel was proof of that. It was like she had to make up for something. And after her first insult, I was freaking obsessed with that full upper lip, as if one taste despite her bitter words would make everything okay. Her eyes were always stormy unless she was reading a stupid book, and her legs dangled so far down when she was in that tree that she'd gotten nicknamed The Jolly Green Giant in school.

That was then. This was…wow.

I crossed the yard and jogged over to her. It was familiar, finding her next to or in the tree. She wore a gorgeous, strappy dress that made you taste summer on your tongue and brought up thoughts I shouldn't have been thinking. Like kissing her, which I'd always known wouldn't happen since her dad was certifiable when it came to his daughter dating. One time, at a parent-teacher conference in high school, I'd sworn I'd overheard some kid in the hall crying because Travis had warned every boy in school to keep it in their pants or he'd send Hazel's great-grandma in to teach them etiquette.

I wasn't sure what dinner and dress etiquette had to do with anything until I realized that half of them had to take it to graduate. And then I had this very extreme nightmare where she had a needle and kept poking things and laughing while the school burned down around her red high heels.

I shuddered. "Yo." I wasn't sure why that was the first word out of my stupid mouth, but I couldn't take it back. The wind had already brought it to her. "Hazel."

Her eyes didn't leave mine as she took a step toward me in her red heels that reminded me of her great-grandma—small kitten heels that could do as much damage as a perfectly pointed stiletto, almost like she was flying incognito for any sad sucker out there who had the balls to hit on her or call her pretty.

I took a step back, then one forward, because…why should I be intimidated? The past was the past, and there was no reason for her to hate me. I was here to—

"You sick, sick, sick…" Okay, why was she repeating *sick* over and over again? And why did I suddenly feel emotionally attacked with a need to sprint back home to my safe space by my motorcycle? "Bastard."

Shit, was she going to grab a heel? She reached for one, then the other. Oh, no. She was going for double or nothing.

Was I snake eyes?

She suddenly dropped them and walked barefoot toward me. "You are the absolute worst. Look, I know you're going through things, too, but you made my life a living hell. And now you have the audacity to be all like, 'Yo, Hazel'?"

She said it like I was one step away from getting a prison tattoo.

I coughed out a curse and forced my best smile. "I mean, I thought it was more or less like a, *yo, Hazel*," I said in a softer, more inviting tone.

She shook her head. Her blond hair was brighter and fell across her shoulders in soft yet aggressive waves. "No, your tone was all, 'Hey, bro, water under the bridge.' Well, the water is firmly,"—she huffed—"firmly…"

I frowned. "Under the bridge. Because the flow of water is technically under the bridge, unless you have a flood, which then means you might lose the bridge, and—"

"Stop, just stop." Tears filled her eyes. "I just graduated, my great-grandma is dead, and I'm celebrating her today. I don't want to fight. Just go home."

"But…" I shoved my hands into my pockets, hoping to look innocent. "I just came to say hi."

"Oh." She smirked and crossed her arms. "To the gross giant?"

I could have sworn every part of my body went numb. "What are you talking about?" Seriously, what was she talking about?

"I know what you said when the rumor started. That I was the gross giant. And you said it to literally every guy in school. But to have you say it? You know, one time I thought we were friends."

"We were frenemies. And not to correct you, but I never said that. Asshole Josh Prichards, who always had a stick up his ass because you turned him down, did."

She looked away and down at the ground where her red shoes lay. Damn, they even looked pretty against the green grass. "Still, you weren't nice."

"Guys are rarely nice when they like someone or find them intriguing," I pointed out as I circled her. "In fact, a lot of times, we default into asshole or stupid mode. It's the most unfair thing in the world because, the minute you want to say, 'I like you,' you end up pulling a ponytail and laughing, or stealing a fruit snack, thinking they'll chase you and ask why so you can get them alone. Wait, that part sounded creepy. I meant adult fruit snacks. This is not first grade. Actually, I'll stop talking now. It went downhill after the snack."

She smiled down at her bare feet. "Doesn't mean I like an asshole."

"Doesn't mean I like a spoiled princess, but…" I walked closer. "At the risk of you biting me or kicking me in the balls, I'm really sorry about your great-grandma. She was special."

She sniffled as her hair fell like a curtain across her face, and all I saw was the upper lip getting bitten. What the hell was wrong with me? "Thanks, but I think it's better if we stay enemies."

I snorted. "You've never dealt with an enemy or a true battle a day in your life."

Her head snapped up, *Exorcist*-style. Later in life, I would say it twisted all the way around until she stared back at me and stole my soul. "What? What was that?"

I liked the fierceness in her eyes, so I took the bait. Maybe that's what love and hate, friendship and being enemies, was all about. "I said"—I gripped her by the chin—"that you've never seen a battle a day in your life."

She smacked my hand away and gave me a shove. "Then I guess you're in for a very long summer of war with the girl next door. You see, that girl is sweet. This one? She's a warrior. And I never back down from a fight. Have a good night."

She grabbed her shoes and stomped off like I didn't understand her. I walked back across the yard with a smile on my face, my first real, genuine smile in a while. She wanted to play?

I was always a fan of games, and I was suddenly an even bigger fan of hers than I was before—not that I hadn't been. She'd rejected me in middle school when I asked to sit by her on the bleachers and offered her my hot Takis while she watched *Stranger Things* on her phone.

Epic fail. She never even heard me; just handed me the bag and kept watching. Saddest Taki moment ever.

After that, it was this weird give-and-take, laugh-and-kind-of-cry sort of relationship. Then, when we got into high school, I grew into my body. She didn't grow into hers. In fact, she got made fun of, and I tried to defend her, but not hard enough. I became a dick and blamed my friends. But I was different now.

Hazel?

She was always just Hazel. The same bright, intelligent, beautiful Hazel. I just wished she saw herself the way everyone else did. Guys were pissed because her dad threatened them in a joking way, and then they were pissed because I was the only one who could talk to her, despite her fascination with Jane Austen.

If she only knew... Wow. I couldn't believe I'd thought that as I returned to my house. Damn social media. She'd been so many guys' Roman Empire—mine included.

But if she wanted a war...

The girl would get a war.

"Yo, Hazel," I called over my shoulder. "Get ready for day one."

She shook her head and kept walking.

She was ill-prepared.

Good.

When I got back into the house, Mom stuttered awake. "Was that

Hazel? Are things good now?"

I grinned as I walked into the living room. "Most excitement I've had in a while. Might get her a graduation present."

"Aw, that's"—she yawned—"so sweet." She tried to get up but stumbled back into the chair. "Sorry, just tired. The meds hit a bit harder today."

With tears in my eyes, I helped her up and wrapped the quilt around her frail shoulders. "We all have those, just rest."

For now, my mind was on my mom. At least, until the next morning, when a present nearly hit me on the way to grabbing the newspaper from the front porch.

I looked down.

It said *TNT* on it.

Very funny.

I shook it like a dumbass.

And it exploded with pink glitter. I found a tiny note inside. *Don't mess with women who wear heels on grass. It takes savage superpowers to walk in a straight line without sinking into the dirt. You've been warned. Also, I always thought men with dirt on their faces needed a bit of pink...maybe go check your motorcycle.*

I flicked the card onto the ground, then picked up some of the pink glitter from my shirt and blew it toward her house. "You have no idea what's coming, little girl."

Chapter Four

"Women are difficult. Their lipstick is their armor, just like their shoes are weapons, and their clothes are their shield."—August Wellington

Hazel

I smiled myself to sleep that night after partying way too long and gifting August pink glitter. In fact, it might have been the best sleep I'd had my entire life.

I stretched my arms over my head and checked my phone.

Only six a.m.?

I still had at least two hours to sleep this off, relax, and just—

The sound of a lawnmower had me jolting up so hard my skull pounded, the pain radiating from the back of my neck to my temples.

"Why?" I croaked, my mouth so dry it hurt to swallow. "Why would someone mow the lawn this early?"

The sound suddenly stopped. Huh, must have been in my head. I curled down around my fluffy, white pillow and started to fall asleep again when the sound of a saw filled the air.

I almost tumbled out of the bed. "The hell?"

Next door, August was sawing down a small tree with the lawnmower still present on the lawn as if he'd thought mid-mow, *"Hey, you know what's a good idea? Tree chopping."*

When he was done with that, he pulled off his black T-shirt and tossed it to the ground. I gaped like the peeping Tom I was and ducked beneath the window ledge, slightly lifting my blackout curtain with my right hand to peek out.

I gasped when he grabbed a bottle of water, poured it over his head, and shook his hair, only to run his hands through the locks and then wipe those same hands down his body.

"Who drinks water like that?" I licked my lips and leaned closer when he suddenly looked over at our house—specifically, my window.

Panicked, I jerked back and dropped the curtain. He didn't see me. I knew he didn't see me.

I squeezed my eyes shut for a few minutes and then slowly crawled back under the covers, only to hear the doorbell ring.

Was everyone awake?

I jolted out of bed and ran down the hall, ready to give whoever it was a piece of my mind, when I saw a small, pink box on the doorstep with my name on it.

It even had a cute white bow with pink and black stripes.

I picked it up, then checked out the scribble on a small piece of white paper.

Not the only thing I had in store for you this morning. Did you like the show? Only the best for the princess.

I immediately scowled, but I was too damn curious not to take the box and its offensive note inside. I quickly tucked the package under my arm, slammed the door behind me, sprinted back up to my room, and leaned against the wall.

What was he up to?

Was the pink glitter too much?

My laugh of disbelief could probably be heard next door. I tossed the box onto my bed and crossed my arms, then heard the lawnmower start again.

I wanted to shout, "*Go to hell!*" out my window. Instead, I looked at the gift again. What? What could it possibly be?

And why?

Would this be a jump scare?

And why did my stomach do a few flip-flops when I thought about the possibility that it actually was a present? I hated him. Loathed him. He was my enemy, not my friend.

I quickly dropped to my knees and drummed my fingertips on the top of the pretty box, then finally convinced myself that it was a stellar idea to untie the pink bow and pull it open. "Here goes nothing."

Weirdly, my hands were shaking, and my pink nail polish stood out as my fingers undid the bow and pulled it loose so I could open the box and look inside.

It was pretty.

And I hated him for it. I hated him so much. Because it was something that my great-grandma would have given me. She'd always called me her little princess, and when I was young, I'd twirl wearing the pink plastic crowns she'd buy at Target, and hold the scepter I believed would control those around me. My parents were good sports, my dad especially. I'd tell him to fall out of the tree house and pretend to be a dog, and he'd actually bark, making me laugh so hard I'd run and get tackled.

I truly had the best upbringing.

My throat swelled as I touched the crown with my fingertips. It was something you'd get from Amazon or another retailer: plastic with fake, silver-framed bright blue diamonds.

With shaking hands, I reached for the note tucked inside.

Spoiled princesses always get crowns, even if they're fake. Should you put yours on? BTW, thanks so much for the glitter, I'll use it wisely.

I tossed the card like it was cursed.

"Take a few breaths," I said out loud. "Just a few deep breaths." It was like I was my own therapist. How dare he take something so personal and turn it into something I should be offended by, all for having an amazing great-grandma and family?

I'd just graduated and celebrated her life, and he sent me this?

I looked over my shoulder at the wall behind me.

It was filled with pictures of me and Great-Grandma Nadine. I was young, but my parents always took pictures when I snuck into her room and opened her makeup drawer. Her lipstick always smelled like vanilla, and she had the tips of the tubes looking funny because of the way she put it on.

It was upside down.

Most people put on lipstick the normal way, where you went in and pressed the tip against your upper lip, facing the lower part downward. She did it the opposite way, and her reasoning made no sense. Weirdly enough, the tip of that lipstick never fell off; it just existed in this weird mold of a thin tower pointing at the bottom of her lip.

"Honey," *she'd said one day after sharing some of her Estee Lauder with me while I watched her do her makeup in her powder room as she sat on her light blue stool, looking in her small mirror. "One day, you'll understand that it doesn't matter*

how you put on lipstick or eyeshadow or if you wear any makeup at all. You do it for you first, always first." She smiled at herself as she rubbed her lips together. "And second? Oh, honey, you do it for your partner. For that person in your life. You want to know why I put on lipstick this way?"

I nodded, in complete awe of her strawberry-red lips and perfect pink blush. Even the blond curls on her head didn't move as she brushed through them.

"You put on lipstick the way you want to live life, against others, upside down, in chaos. You live life because it's meant to be lived and experienced. You don't go with the norm—there's no fun in that. You wear your heels proudly, your sneakers with honor, and you put on lipstick however the heck you please.

"At the end of the day, you become a person who goes against the grain, someone who can flip her lipstick upside down, put it on, and smile. Life is short. Chaos is welcome because it brings in so many factors. And, honey, my only goal for you is to know that no matter what path it takes you on—you can pave your own way and do it with authority. My lipstick proves that time and time again."

She smiled down at the lipstick with its thin, upside-down tip. "Do you know I've never had a lipstick wear out or break by putting it on this way?" She showed me the small black container, her pink nails shining against it. "I think it's the universe telling me that maybe all of us can do things our own way. It's just sometimes so much easier to follow the crowd. Be your own crowd." She looked down at me and pinched my cheek. "Wear lipstick however you want. Now, put it on."

I grabbed the lipstick and, with shaking hands, twisted it across my lips. Then I turned it upside down just like she did and smacked my lips together because, if anyone had it right...

It was Great-Grandma Nadine.

I dropped the crown to the floor and stood. "How dare you?"

He wasn't there to hear me, but I heard the lawnmower so, with my pajamas still on—little pink Hello Kitty shorts and a mismatched green shirt—I ran outside, my fluffy orange Garfield slippers in place. Maybe later I'd realize that the Garfield on my left foot was missing an eye, and the one on the right had no tail, but whatever.

I marched next door, sleep mask pulled up and all—that one was slightly more embarrassing since it said: *I dream of tacos*, but I had no time to think.

August didn't even notice me, so the only thing I could think to do was throw a Garfield slipper at his face and say, "Sorry." And to be clear, I felt bad for one-eyed Garfield, not August.

Never. August.

The slipper hit him in the back of the head. He slowly stopped mowing and turned. Why the hell was he so good-looking, even while sweaty? It was like he'd just oiled himself up and was like, "*Oh, might go to a body-building competition but can't decide if I did enough on leg day or carb loaded yet.*"

His golden abs seriously had the worst timing as the sun rose and decided to bless him like baby Jesus or Simba from *The Lion King*, just shining down across all freaking fifteen of them. Okay, there weren't fifteen, but again, I didn't care. It was glorious, and I hated him even more for the crown in that moment. It was sinister, like he knew.

"You." I pointed with my finger.

He held up his hands. "Is lawn care illegal?"

No, but abs like that should be, you asshole.

"NO!" I roared, then reached for the other slipper and held it high. "I'll use it, don't make me use it, August."

He raised his toned, muscular, god-like golden right arm and ran his fingertips through his thick, sweaty hair, pulling it away from his green eyes. "Are you threatening me with Garfield?"

"If I must, *Odie.*"

He dropped his arm and burst out laughing. His dimples were on full display. "I'm the dumb dog, but aren't you the one obsessed with carbs? Should I bring a lasagna next time?"

I loved lasagna. How dare he? "NO!" I roared. My parents were half-Italian, but again, not the point. "Just apologize, and this weird war can end. I'm only here for a few months before I start work anyway."

"Ah, work. Do you know the meaning, or is it just like this thing you think about at night when you get spoon-fed meals by a chef and count the money in your bank account?"

If there were any witnesses, they'd probably say that I growled at his response instead of in my head, but I took a deep breath and said, "Fine. Fine. Say what you will, but this is over. That was a low blow. And you saw my crowns before. You knew it was a thing."

He suddenly frowned. "What? What thing?"

"Great-Grandma!" I spat.

He kept that stupid look of confusion on his face, which left me no choice but to grab the hose next to his foot and aim it at him. "Don't make me."

"Wet?" He shook his head. "Look, it was a total joke because you're a little princess. I thought you'd laugh, not attack me with water and a Garfield slipper. Come on, you gave me glitter. Tit for tat. We should be even."

I never understood the concept of seething, but I felt it. I felt it in that moment as my fingers clutched the nozzle of the hose. "Apologize."

"Did we just go from *Garfield* to *Venom*? I'm confused."

"Huh?"

"Apologize," he yelled, spreading his buff arms wide as he stood by the lawnmower. The cut grass smelled so fresh that morning that I hated him even more because I automatically felt better about life. "Apologize. You know, how like in the *Venom* movie, he keeps yelling because Eddie keeps offending him and…" He stopped talking. "Not a fan of movies, or?"

"Aghhhh." I dropped the slipper to the ground and shoved it on. "Give me my other Garfield and I'll leave. But know this isn't over. You know what you did."

He smirked, the corner of his mouth tilting up to the right as he leaned down and grabbed the cartoon cat. Then, as if in slow motion, he walked over to me and knelt. "Up."

"Huh?"

"Your foot. I mean, it's technically a slipper…" He held out one-eyed Garfield like it was a prize. "Right?"

I lifted my foot. He slowly slipped the fluffy thing on and stood.

"I'm still angry."

He tilted his head, then with shaking fingers, reached for my chin and held it between his fingertips. For whatever reason, I didn't pull away. "Sometimes, we need to be angry first in order to be happy. So, let yourself be angry. I was just kidding, but if it got this reaction out of you where I get to see a face mask, Garfield, and whatever the hell you're wearing, I might just do it more."

"Don't."

"Will." He nodded. "Now, go back and shower. You have mascara streaks down your face. God, did you even wash up before bed last night? Also, mirrors, they exist, use them."

He was teasing, I knew it, but I was too hurt and raw to see it. "I loathe you. Just wait."

"Aw, princess. With bated breath."

He turned and started the lawnmower while I stood there like an idiot. As I stomped back to the house looking like a nightmare, a small smile formed on my lips.

He wanted to play?

Well, games could be hazardous, and I would not be outdone by lawnmower boy.

Let's. Go.

Chapter Five

"When Garfield becomes your Iron Man."—*Hazel Titus*

August

Was it wrong to be excited after seeing a sad, pathetic Garfield slipper and a half-asleep girl yelling at me?

Probably.

Maybe that meant you'd hit rock bottom. Regardless, I was literally smiling all morning when I went into the living room and saw Mom sleeping on the couch. I grabbed the red and blue quilt, pulled it up to her neck, and kissed her forehead—*just to make sure.*

God, it sucked to even think that.

To make sure.

What? That she wasn't cold?

My good mood left until I looked back at the lawn.

"Mmmm." Mom stirred. "You talked with Hazel this morning. Were you yelling?"

I smirked. "Pretty sure she did all the yelling, Mom."

Her laugh had always been one of my favorite things about her. It was always too loud, boisterous to the point that when we went to the movies, people stared at her, and I would sink into the seat like I was a part of it. But now? I wished it was like that again and didn't sound so weak and frail.

"August." Her lips pressed together like she was gaining energy from not speaking before she opened her mouth again. "Yelling doesn't always mean fighting. If you evoked a response in her, maybe that's a good thing. God knows I would do anything in this world to see you happy and with someone before…"

"No." I rushed to her side. "Before what? Aliens come? Zombies? Before In-N-Out takes notice? Nope, not happening. Just relax, you're tired. I'll deal with her. It's just some friendly, um…banter."

"Exactly how you were born." Coughing ended the argument as she turned on her side and went back to sleep.

For the rest of the night, I stared up at the ceiling.

What would have happened if I'd grabbed Hazel by the waist back then and told her how pretty I thought she was despite my anger that she didn't realize it?

The way she stared at me was all venom.

Ironic.

The way I stared back at her was all antidote.

But she never saw it that way because she never saw herself how others should see her—the way her family saw her.

As precious.

Something to fight for. Someone to protect. Someone to also annoy, because there was nothing better than someone who fought for something without sitting down. I wanted that for my future.

I jolted awake and rubbed my hands down my face. "Nope, no. Nope. Not thinking about family. I'm young, so young. Ha, ha, nightmares. Is Mom smoking weed and suddenly getting everyone in the house high and delirious, thinking all the thoughts?" Voice weak and raspy, I lay back down and turned onto my side. Her window was right there. The light was on.

I shook my head. "What could she possibly do to make me mad?"

I hated myself a bit for turning onto my side and staring back at her illuminated window across the yard, wondering if she would crawl up that tree or lie in bed.

What was she doing?

Was she the same Hazel I remembered? She seemed stronger, angrier. And I liked it more because a weak Hazel made me want to hold her. A strong Hazel made me want to fight for her, and I wanted to fight more than I wanted to hold because that meant she was strong.

And I needed someone strong.

Because every time my mom coughed, I felt weak.

Every time I heard her laugh, a part of my laugh died a bit.

People are people. In the end, we all want a shoulder to cry on, someone to laugh with. Or, at the very least, someone who won't just stand by our side but shove us behind them and say, "*I've got this.*"

God, what would that even feel like?

It was the last thought I had before random knocking filled the air and I heard the chicken—or wait, rooster? Who the hell had a rooster? And why? Why at this hour? Why? We weren't in the country. We both had houses by the freaking Columbia River. Did they suddenly release random roosters and chickens to entertain the ducks and fish?

My imagination. Obviously.

I yawned and closed my eyes again.

The rooster sounded.

Again.

I jolted awake and rubbed my blurry eyes, attempting to focus on the white wall in my room. Suddenly, I heard it to my left. Slowly, I turned and saw an honest to God rooster in my front yard. "The hell?"

It wouldn't shut up.

I had no pellet gun, but I wouldn't lie about it or to myself. If I had one, I would have been tempted to use it and then cook the thing…wait, could you even eat a rooster?

Was that inhumane?

Probably. I did live in Portland, after all. Animals had rights, and we were within city limits. I'd learned last year when we had wild turkeys roaming and eating people's gardens that, apparently, it was frowned upon to hunt for Thanksgiving. Who knew? But going to the store…totally fine.

I could deal with the rooster once I had coffee and did a jumping jack or two. Whatever.

I rolled out of bed and put my feet onto the cold hardwood, swearing both pinky toes almost cramped. Going back to bed sounded like the best idea ever, but I knew Mom would be up—not because of the rooster but because mornings had always been her thing. And while my dad was gone, it was my job to get her ready, perch her in front of the window to watch life pass her by, and fill up her coffee cup. While it sounded depressing, it was actually the highlight of her days.

"Look." She pointed at the school bus that'd pulled up down the street. "Leslie's six now. Wow, she's gotten so big. And those brown pigtails. Aren't her pink bows adorable?"

"Yeah," I agreed. I always agreed because, in my world, my mom was right. She *was* my world, what kept it spinning.

"Oh." She swatted me weakly. "Did you know that Hazel's going to start working at her dad's ranch soon? She's taking over as the main bookkeeper while she gets her MBA. So wonderful. Aren't you proud?"

Of sparkle queen? Yeah, maybe. Sort of. "Yup," I answered. "So proud."

A knock suddenly sounded at the door.

Mom rested a weak hand on my arm, her small diamond from Dad still shining under the lights of the room. "Get that, will you?"

"As if I'd let you race me," I teased, swallowing the lump in my throat. Her skin was paler today, and I knew I'd been helping with her meds and getting her to sleep as much as possible. But I needed Dad to come back. Not because I wanted a break—I would spend every moment with her—it was just…I didn't want to fail.

Failure as soon as she got sick became my kryptonite, not just in life but also in friendships. The fear of letting people down. My biggest insecurity was not being what people expected and falling short.

Her hand dropped, and her head turned to the side as she sighed and fell asleep again. Our morning ritual was done. Now, it was time to get the mail or package or whatever had been delivered.

The floor creaked as I walked over and reached for the bronze door handle. Our house was expensive and in a prestigious part of Portland, so we didn't have knobs. Instead, we had this weird giant handle that made you feel like you were in a castle and not the suburbs by the river.

I shoved it down and looked out.

A simple brown box sat on the doorstep, and it was addressed to me. I was leery after the rooster had somehow planted itself on our property, but I assumed that was probably Hazel's weird prank. A rooster. Congrats, it worked.

I shook the box, and my head was all like, "*Oh, you know, just in case it's a bomb,*" not thinking far enough ahead that if it *were* a bomb, I would be dead.

All men are idiots, apparently.

I even shook it again after that errant thought and then started pulling away the tape, only to open it and see a simple black razor with a note.

Nobody wants to marry the Beast in real life. They only tolerate him for the library. Shave that scratch before you end up alone. Oh, and even if you had a library…—Garfield-wearing Hazel

I picked up the razor and clutched it in my hand

I'd like to say the war ended there.

But what followed was a constant battle of wills.

The next Friday, Hazel woke up to find *Jane Eyre* with instructions on how to read books. I was very detailed.

She followed that up with three types of organic soap because she said I looked like I'd never used it a day in my life.

I followed that up with crickets in her house. Okay, not a proud moment, but I was at a loss for something to continue this weird banter because at least it distracted me from my mom's failing health and my dad's return, where he'd most likely see her and collapse in front of me. Meaning I had to take care of everyone physically and emotionally. I wasn't really sure I had a lot left to do that.

I was already struggling, so I focused on the girl next door, her hate for me, and her cute way of showing it.

After the crickets, though, things went deathly silent. A worry for sure. My mom even asked what was next, and all I could give her was, "The apocalypse. Brace yourself."

A week later, I came to the conclusion that she was either bored or gave up. It annoyed me that the last thing I saw when I closed my eyes was her light shutting off as if I were off, too.

Gone.

Forgotten.

Chapter Six

"Note to self: Women have memories of steel. Damn Bigfoot."—*August Wellington*

Hazel

I would end him.

And wait until it was dark.

Was I losing it? Probably. Was this fun? Absolutely. Every time he opened a gift or saw a prank, I laughed and wondered why he didn't just straight up come over and say something. Instead, he just responded.

It became our summer game, and while I loathed how I was treated and made fun of in high school, I kind of loved the attention now.

Maybe it would last a month or two. Perhaps it would end. But for the next few weeks, he was my hazard to hold, and I'd take it to my grave.

The clincher after he sent me the book, and I sent him special soap, was a pink princess blanket. You'd think it wasn't a big deal, but it had Disney princesses all over it. I didn't even care if he didn't know, but my great-grandma always told me to pick one, whatever princess I wanted to be. I was allowed to be her and changed my mind often, so looking at that blanket with literally every princess on it made me feel like he was crawling inside my psyche and trying to mess with me. Maybe that was why I went off the deep end. Who knew?

It had been a few days, and I knew he was antsy—not that I was stalking him or anything. But I saw the curtains pulled, and glanced from the tree when he went to the side yard and stared at our house like he was guarding his property against me.

So, to throw him off, I took a few days off to retaliate. This time, I knew I'd get him good.

He'd always had a fear of Bigfoot. I wasn't sure why other than that it was rumored to be in the Pacific Northwest. So, I splurged and went on Amazon to buy a Bigfoot costume. All I needed was to sneak into the house or climb up to his window. But when I put the costume on, it was too big, so it was hard to see through the eyes. Not to mention that it smelled like rubber inside the mask, and if any hunter saw me, they'd probably shoot me on sight for both meat and glory. But whatever, I could run fast.

Once my parents were asleep, I shoved the mask on and stared into the mirror. Oddly enough, I looked like a cross between a gorilla and a man with a bit of dinosaur dropped in.

My zip-in costume was covered in plastic fur, I had gloves with claws, and my mask was huge over my head. I nearly tripped over the threshold when I tried to quietly close the door. Ohhhh, *that's* why I felt like a dinosaur. I had T-Rex arms that flapped in the wind as I ran across the yard and crouched in front of his house.

Dad had their code since we're friendly neighbors like that, so typing it in was nothing. 2021? Okay, who had such an easy passcode?

I typed it in and…success.

It flashed green.

Perfection.

I slowly crept across the floor. His dad wasn't home until next week, at least according to my sources, and his mom was asleep. And August? Oh, he'd be upstairs in his room, sleeping soundly until I scared the crap out of him.

Man, I wished I had a partner in crime to take a picture of him shitting the bed, but alas, all I would have was the memory of his fear.

I slowly crawled up the stairs on my hands and knees, still nearly blind from the mask slipping, and made it to the final step. It creaked as my right paw hit it. Wincing, I looked around as much as I could out half my right eye and waited, my breathing labored.

Nothing happened.

Smirking behind my plastic mask, I crept along the hall until I found his room. His door was open. Aw, he was sleeping soundly, a lump in the bed, though I couldn't see his face again on account of my stupid costume. Still, this would be incredible.

I crawled into his room and leaned by the side of the bed. This was my moment, my crescendo. I stood to my full height and raised my paws into the air, only to feel a searing pain as I collapsed against the bed and was forced onto my back while a body fell on top of me. "Stop or I'll call the police."

A muffled "Huh?" came out of my mask. "Why the police?"

"Intruder. And my dad's a retired cop so you should probably settle down, you sick creep. Who dresses like this and sneaks into people's homes?"

This was the part where I probably shouldn't have raised my hand, but I did.

He slapped it away. "Seriously? What's wrong with you?"

"YOU!" I roared. "You're what's wrong. And I can read. Well, in fact." I just couldn't let go of that note he'd left with *Jane Eyre*.

His green eyes squinted briefly before he tugged off my mask and threw it to the floor. "Hazel?"

"Surprised?"

Lips pressed together, he sighed. "Wish I was, but actually, no. No, I'm not surprised."

"Liar, you were terrified."

"Nope, just trying to abide by the law when it comes to someone trespassing on private property. You're lucky I didn't tase you."

"Aw, you need a Taser? Can't even use your fists?"

"I can use my fists."

"It's okay." I patted him on the shoulder, then squeezed as much as I could with my plastic claws. "Some men just can't use things. Admit it, you're one of them."

"I admit nothing." He pushed me down against the mattress. "And you smell like melted plastic."

"Some might call that romantic."

"Some might call you psychotic."

I stuck out my tongue. "You started this battle, but I'm pretty sure I'm winning the war. Now, I can sleep in peace."

"Bet you have a teddy bear," he taunted, still on top of me.

I laughed and leaned up, so close to his face that I could see the flecks of gold in his green eyes. "Bet you're a virgin."

His nostrils flared. "Bet you've never had a good kiss in your entire life."

"Bet you don't even know how."

"Challenge accepted." He leaned down so aggressively there was no way I could stop the onslaught of his perfect mouth before it pressed against mine. My hands had ideas of their own as they tried to pull at his hair while my lips parted for him.

His groan literally gave me no choice but to follow suit as my hands—aka gloves—stroked the back of his neck. It was a good, deep kiss. Such a good kiss that I hated him even more for proving me wrong.

His tongue slid into my mouth and then, sheer pain again, this time in the form of what felt like electrocution as I went limp beneath him.

"Are you okay!?" a male voice shouted. "I heard groaning. Holy shit, is that a bear?"

"Dad." August jumped up, then sat back down, pulling a blanket over his lap. "What the hell?"

"I thought you were getting mauled."

"I was doing the mauling. Her fault. And now you've tased her."

What? I'd been tased? My shaky eyes looked over at my arm and leg. Oh, look at that…tased. Was my tongue supposed to feel so heavy?

"You can't just go around tasing people. We've talked about this. Innocent until proven guilty," August yelled again. "I don't hate her enough to tase her."

"Well…" His dad put his weapon away. "Obviously not since her tongue was down your throat. Or vice versa. You know, there are better ways to tell a girl you like her."

Hear, hear.

Still couldn't talk.

His dad leaned against the wall. "Son, you don't need to pull her hair or throw rocks, send a note in class, or ask her to circle things then hold hands at skate night—"

"Oh, God, here we go," August muttered under his breath, still sitting next to my lifeless body. "I know, Dad. I'm a full-ass grown adult."

His dad looked at me, then at August, then back at me. He wasn't wearing a shirt, only red pajama bottoms and a black baseball hat that said, *Yee-Haw*. I mean, for a dad, he looked pretty fit. Good for him. He even had some marginally attractive chest hair.

I'd give him a thumbs-up, but my situation was dire, and I had no life in my bones.

August's dad looked between us again. "Yes, clearly you are a full-ass grown adult who, according to Travis—one of my best friends, mind you—has been on some weird prank-hate war with Hazel." He did a double take. "Oh, God. Hazel?"

"Mhiiiii." I tried to speak, but it came out sounding like *I'm high*. Not the best start.

"You're Bigfoot."

He said it like it was true, like the actual myth had just been solved. At that point, what did someone do but nod?

So, I did.

He sighed. "I'm calling your dad. This prank war stops now. In fact, no…" He started walking away, then turned back around. "You guys settle this without us. We have enough stress." He didn't say it, but I knew he meant his wife. "Enough stress," he said again. "Without dealing with whatever the hell you guys have going on here. Pack up. You'll get the Jeep, August. Solve whatever the hell issues you guys have in the mountains. When you come back, you'd better actually be functioning adults in society."

"Dad," August piped up. "We are. This has nothing to do with anything but her being a spoiled princess and me making some jokes."

"And…" I just had to have the last word, didn't I? "He was mean to me in high school."

Oh, wow. That was literally all I had.

Both stared at me while I sat there in a stupid costume with plastic folding and melting into my skin. I even had one weird claw on my right hand held up like I had an actual point to make, other than the fact that I had crept into their house in a full Bigfoot costume just to get the upper hand.

Ha, hand. See? Get it?

I hung my head. "Sorry."

"Six. It's six a.m.!" his dad shouted. "In the morning. Get your shit together, you're going camping, and you're working out whatever the hell is going on. Touch some grass, look at deer, see nature, get eaten by a bear, I don't care. Maybe we did you guys wrong raising you in the city. Do you even know where your food comes from?" He sighed. "Never mind. Just go, go, go, go. And, Hazel, if I see that costume again, I'm burning it."

"Agreed," August said under his breath.

I sneered at him, then immediately looked at his dad and felt a weird need to bow. "Sorry."

"Go," he said again. "And I'm calling your dad, damn it. You guys are in your twenties but act like you're still in middle school. Stupid baby boomers did every generation wrong after them. The hell?"

I hung my head as I passed him and walked home. I knew I was in trouble when my dad opened the door after I stepped onto the grass by the tree.

His arms were folded. Mom was next to him, and my sixteen-year-old brother was eating ice cream and eyeing me with judgmental eyes.

Yeah, I was in deep shit.

And now, I was going camping with the enemy.

"Inside, Bigfoot. NOW!" Dad roared.

He didn't have to ask me twice.

Chapter Seven

"Road trips are for the strong. Coffee is for the weak."—Hazel Titus

August

"I'm driving," I announced. "No way in hell do I trust you to operate a motor vehicle after sneaking into my house at six a.m. with a Bigfoot costume on, then mauling me with your face."

Scared the shit out of me. I would take it to my grave. The plastic claws would haunt me for an eternity. How did it look so real? Maybe I was just hallucinating, but it wasn't a cool prank. I mean, I was in until that moment, then I was just straight up like…nope, tapping out, not fun. Yet she kept it going.

Honestly, how did we even get into this situation? As adults and college graduates—at least, in her case—where and how the hell did our summer turn into a prank war? Normally, I'd say it was stupidity or boredom, but I wasn't even sure anymore. All I knew was that our parents were pissed, and we had to bury whatever hatchet we had between us and make it work.

On top of that, part of me wondered if Dad just wanted some time with Mom without me. If so, I couldn't be mad about that. I would do the same, so it wasn't hard to convince me to leave with Satan.

I'd do anything for my parents.

The doctor had said Mom had maybe a few months left. Now that Dad was back, it was time—giving time and spending it until the end.

My chest ached. I wouldn't be selfish. I'd had time with her, and I knew no miracle would come from Heaven. As did she. I just wanted her every moment to be special—not for me, but for her. She deserved it.

I took a deep breath then jerked my head to the right. "Say what?"

"You mauled me with your mouth." Hazel crossed her arms and unexpectedly pointed out the kiss that I did not daydream about several times while packing up the Jeep. "And participated."

"Yes. I made out with Bigfoot. I'll be sure to put that on my tombstone after you kill me," I ground out. "It will be right up there with getting a root canal and walking barefoot in the snow while being chased by a bear."

"I might," she muttered.

"What?"

"Kill you." Damn, harsh. I almost laughed.

"Cool, sounds good. I mean, at this rate, we both might die on this camping trip. Do you even know what a tent is?" She didn't. I would die on that hill. She probably thought it was this thin little thing you poked into the ground that protected you at all costs, not realizing you needed food, water, blankets, and any other survival gear she probably couldn't even spell because, again, silver-spoon-fed princess. I liked her, she was pretty, she'd been nice for a while, and I'd felt bad for her. But now? Now, she just seemed stuck up and oblivious to how the world worked around her.

She swallowed like she was suddenly nervous and adjusted her blond ponytail before tapping her right pointer finger against her lips. I hated that I fixated on those lips. I blamed it on the fact that mine had been on hers during some weird shift in the universe. It didn't matter. All we had to do was survive this. "A tent provides protection from the elements."

"Protection, my ass. Even a condom isn't one hundred percent," I muttered and started the engine to my black Jeep. "Let's just make the parents happy so they don't murder us and then pretend everything is fine and that you don't hate me so we can go back home, and I can take care of—"

I stopped talking.

Because my only purpose was my mom.

Hazel's only purpose was to succeed at all costs and become something—something I would never be. Because when someone in your life was sick—your family, someone you loved—you only saw a haze. You didn't see yourself. It was just this glimpse of fog that you hoped you would make it through but knew you probably wouldn't. And then you got terrified that when or if you did, you'd have nothing left but emptiness. No purpose.

"Just go," Dad had said. "I need to take care of Mom... I want—" He hesitated. I hated when he did that, like he was weighing his next words and trying to protect me from something—just like that stupid tent. "I want time and selfishly get all of that if you go end this little war-bet thing with the girl you refuse to admit you like."

"I don't like her," I said, way too hard and fast. Anyone could see through it. I'd loved our kiss. She was pretty—violent, yes, but just something I wanted for myself after sacrificing everything for others. Someone to make me feel alive because I'd been watching what I loved die for years, seeing it slowly fading in front of me, only to one day disappear.

Dad smirked. "Yeah, okay. So whoever gets back and gives up this little prank war this summer and concedes wins. I don't care if it's you or her. What I care about is..." He looked back at my mom sleeping on the couch. "I care about her, and I know I've been gone a lot, but I really want to spend some time with her without you. I don't mean that in a hurtful way, it's just...life is sometimes spent so often with family and kids, and everyone wants to be together, but there comes a point in time where you want to go back to the past. Where it was just you and the person you fell for. Where you can lie to yourself and say everything's going to be the same if you just have that other person by your side. I know she's sick. I know we don't have a lot of time. But with the time we have left, it would be"—tears streamed down his cheeks—"a gift, I think, to just be with her in love while you go battle in war. Is that okay?"

The fact that he'd even asked me for permission was enough.

The fact that he'd made perfect sense made it even harder.

They were going to have a honeymoon before the funeral. Depressing, inspiring, call it whatever you wanted.

And I couldn't be angry that he selfishly wanted that time with his wife. Given the choice, I would do the same.

"Fine." Hazel jolted me out of my thoughts and buckled her seat belt, snapping it into its spot with finality. "Let's just go. Let's camp, explore wildlife. Maybe we can befriend a fox and then come back and tell everyone how magical it was." She pushed her hands together. "We could burst out in song. I mean, a small one, nothing too crazy, and then boom, we go our separate ways, everyone's happy, and the dads don't take away all the things we need to survive. Done."

"I'm already surviving," I pointed out as we pulled out of the driveway. I mentally made a checklist of all the supplies we had and what we still needed to pick up. Hazel thought this was some sort of lying down of arms, when really, I knew what it actually was.

An excuse for my dad to have one last moment with my mom.

I'd let Hazel believe it was because of her weird costume and pranks, but I knew my dad had seen an opening, an opportunity, the minute he came home. Assuming my dad was as close to hers as he claimed, Travis likely felt the same way.

Sending your kids away so you could have special moments with your soulmate before everyone came back and prepared for the worst.

I shook the dark thoughts from my head. "You're milking."

"A cow?" she shrieked.

"No, life," I deadpanned.

"I'm not. I went to college, I graduated, I'm going to start working and—"

"Did you pay for it? College? Did you even think for one second how hard it is for others to even *go* to college, let alone sit there all smug like—"

"She died!" Hazel yelled, making me suddenly swerve into oncoming traffic as I tried to pull onto the highway. "My great-grandma died while I was trying to pass my last business class to graduate, so don't preach to me about how hard things are. Yes, it's hard financially for a lot of people, but don't for one second forget how hard it is for those who go through emotional trauma while trying to survive. Now, drive."

"Finally." I hit the accelerator, ignoring how her words hit so deeply that I felt as if she'd bruised my chest. She knew my mom was sick. She had no clue how bad things were or that we'd been given such a short time before she passed unless a miracle happened.

One thing I could appreciate about our doctor was that he was always brutally honest. I'd rather be given the truth than a lie that would leave me unaware. And unprepared.

I cleared my throat. I was uncomfortable and suddenly emotional. I almost wished the stupid costume was back. "That's something we can agree on. The emotional trauma is worse. It's always worse."

"Like anxiety," she agreed.

"Like knowing you can do nothing but have to keep trying."

"Because if you stop..." She sniffed. "It means they died in vain."

"Yeah."

"Yeah." She looked out the window. "Keep driving. I'm going to close my eyes. Try to go in straight lines, August."

"I color outside of them."

Her eyes were closed, but she smiled and hugged her chest with her arms. "Yeah, this is my shocked face."

"It's a pretty face."

"Was that a compliment from my high school nemesis?"

"Never." I grinned and hit the accelerator. "I'll wake you up when we stop at the store before the campsite I normally go to. I hope you packed warm."

"Blankets and jackets." She yawned. "Oh, and a light stick. I grabbed one of those."

"To throw at the bear when it attacks you or what?"

She didn't answer. Within seconds, she was already asleep, her head lolling to the side. Smiling, I reached over and gently pushed her toward the door so she could rest against something, then jerked my hand away.

No. Just no. She was pretty, and sometimes she was nice when she wasn't trying to sneak into my house or offend me, but she wasn't for me.

I sometimes wondered if I would ever have enough actual space in my heart to take someone else on. Other times, I was reminded that the minute my mom died, I'd have a vacancy, but it was more like a foreclosure on my soul. One that said nothing would ever exist there again and nobody would want to buy it.

What was dead and gone was dead and gone, and sometimes it was best to leave memorials for those people rather than risk getting hurt by filling the hole and losing someone all over again.

I'd keep the rooms empty.

I'd keep the lights on somehow.

And I'd remember.

It was the best I could do.

Chapter Eight

"No human has any business looking cute while they sleep. It just goes against the laws of nature."—August Wellington

Hazel

I didn't even realize I'd fallen asleep until I woke up with a sore neck, a weird-looking red plaid blanket across my lap, and a Jeep still running but missing its driver.

I rubbed my eyes and looked over at the empty black leather seat August had been sitting in before personal abandonment. August was missing. I hadn't even heard him leave the car let alone shut the door.

The keys were still in the ignition, and we were in front of an Albertsons grocery store in the mountains.

It was pretty. I mean, Portland was already technically in a mountainous area, but this place was closer to Seaside and Tillamook. Nestled right on the Oregon coast, it had rocky cliffs that dropped directly into tumultuous waters. On top of that, it had this beautiful fog that made you think you were in a fairy tale, being both on the beach and in the trees.

I shivered and turned on the heat. How was it so much colder two hours away from the city?

I didn't have to wait long. In his tight, white long-sleeve shirt and jeans, August was already rushing toward the Jeep with two bags in his hands. Please, let those be snacks. I was starving.

He opened the back and shoved the bags in, then returned to the front and opened his door, looking at me. "Good nap?"

My eyes narrowed. "Your smile feels judgmental."

"That's because it is. Oh, and you had some drool earlier, so I just ended up grabbing an empty coffee cup and holding it under your jaw with one hand. Too bad you can't recycle spit. You'd have a good thing going."

I yawned. "Not even your sarcasm or insults can ruin my good mood right now." I stretched my arms over my head. "That was probably the best nap I've had in years."

"Naps. I wonder what that's actually like. You know, resting one's eyes, not waking up with severe panic attacks and anxiety over everything you have to do that day or what might come tomorrow and—" He stopped talking. "Sorry, when I'm tired, my censor just dies a slow death in my mouth, and all the words come out."

I was a bit stunned he'd said all of that, so I just shrugged. "It happens to the best of us. What did you get?"

Good, solid subject change.

"Beans. I figure if I eat enough, I can drive you out of your tent as prey for the wild animals."

"I think your scent would be enough to keep them far, far away from our campsite. And you know you shouldn't talk about farting if you want to look marginally attractive to any sex."

He put the SUV into drive. "Oh, don't worry. The idea is to repel, not attract."

"Animals?"

"You." He grinned. "Now, let's go set up. I have a spot right near Canon Beach that lets you have tents on the outskirts near the woods. It's nice, and bonus, I've never been mauled by any wild creatures."

"Yay." I did a sad fist pump in the air. "Let's just get this over with, bury the hatchet, give the parents some alone time, and then go back home. How long are we camping again?"

"Dad said three days." August's voice cracked, and then he cleared his throat and went extremely silent—the tense sort of silence you knew was necessary without even knowing the reasons why.

I didn't say anything for the next twenty minutes. The view was pretty enough, and I was still groggy from my nearly two-hour nap. It was already starting to get dark by the time we made it to the campsite, or at least what I assumed was the campsite. There were two RVs, a tent, and a fire going, but that was basically it. I could hear the waves crashing before we got out of the Jeep. August remained silent as he killed the engine and slammed his door. There were no bathrooms that I could see, which meant I had a date with nature and a very embarrassing talk with August about where to go to the bathroom to look forward to. Fingers crossed there'd be no curious bears.

I left my purse and phone in the Jeep so I could help, then pulled my black hoodie over my head and shivered. I was glad I'd packed more than one sweatshirt and a big jacket just in case it rained.

August was pulling stuff out of the back of the SUV: two blue folding chairs, some dry firewood that he moved to the side, some food, and finally, the tent. He left the blankets inside just in case. Wait, why was there only one tent?

I stared, then stared harder. "That looks small."

"What?" He swatted away my pointed finger. "There aren't any spiders or bugs. What's your deal?" I pointed again, and he swatted again, then cursed. "Seriously, what's your issue? Have you really never seen a tent before?"

First off, it was yellow—bright yellow. NASA would have no trouble finding us, just like every other creature, Bigfoot included. "Why is it so small-looking?"

He stared at it, then back at me, then back at it. "Because it's for one person. Maybe two total if you spoon the hell out of each other. But don't worry, princess. You'll be in your tent. Everything's fine."

In that moment, I didn't think I would ever be able to adequately describe the actual panic that stripped my soul and humanity. "Um, my tent?"

You know when you know you're completely screwed, and your body kind of goes numb, but your hands manage to prickle all over while a cold chill rests on your skin? And then you get those bad goose bumps, not the good ones that tell you you're about to be kissed or pressed against a wall with your hair pulled in a really good way? That. That was this feeling.

"Yes." He rolled his eyes. "Your tent. It was right next to the third chair on the ground and the extra sleeping bag your dad left for you."

"Ha ha." It wasn't funny. "The extra sleeping bag?"

His green eyes furrowed. "Yes, to sleep in, unless you planned on wrapping yourself up in a blanket and sleeping on the sand under the stars."

"I didn't bring it," I blurted.

His yellow, bundled-up tent dropped to the ground. "I'm sorry, what? Because it sounded like you just said you didn't bring it. Define *it*. I need to know what it is."

I gulped and hugged my body. "It would be more like a plural word in this scenario?"

"How plural? And why is that a question? It should be a statement, like…oh, I forgot my bug spray, or my phone. My charger. I forgot my favorite bag of chips. What did you not bring, Hazel?"

"I was distracted." I sidestepped the question. "And may have forgotten to put my tent and the extra sleeping bag in the Jeep."

Had he yelled, I would have felt much better. Instead, he just stared at me like he was about to throw the tent and leave me to fend for myself. "So, you're saying you forgot what you needed for the camping trip?"

"Look." I spread my arms wide. "It's not a big deal. I can sleep in the Jeep."

He burst out laughing. "You're going to sleep in the SUV and freeze to death at night? Do you realize how cold it gets? And we aren't keeping the Jeep on all night. The tent holds body heat, and we put it in front of a fire. Do you even know how nature works, or is it just a guess from reading at this point?"

I rolled my eyes. "I know what you mean, but how cold is it actually supposed to get tonight?"

Rain started to come down as the wind picked up.

I was already shivering.

He grabbed his tent. "Come on, help me put this up, and we'll figure the rest out. Don't grab the firewood yet, and leave the dry blankets."

I huffed and followed him toward the edge of the tree line. He pointed up at the large trees. "If we camp here, it shouldn't get too windy, and we can at least have a fire. The farther we get toward the ocean, the windier it gets. Normally, this area is calmer, but early summer storms can be a thing here, especially with the rain."

I nodded like I knew exactly what he was talking about. He dropped the tent to the ground and started pulling pieces out of the bag. "Just tell me how I can help."

He snorted out a laugh. "I would tell you to read the instructions, but it would just take longer. Why don't you start setting up the chairs and build a place for the fire, as in put rocks in a small circle, dig out a dry hole, and put in the firewood? Then grab the poop shovel and—"

"The what shovel?" I asked.

He sighed like I was the most annoying person on the planet and turned, hands on his narrow hips. Why did jeans have to look so good on him? And why did his stupid thighs match the tree trunks next to him? "For the bathroom."

"A bathroom shovel? But you called it a poop shovel."

"Oh, I'm sorry, I'll use better words. The poo or potty shovel. Grab it from the back so if you have to use the bathroom in the middle of the night, you already have a hole dug out so you can bury your surprise in nature."

His grin was menacing, all straight, white teeth mocking me.

"But…" I sniffled. "I mean, I've camped before, but there were always bathrooms close by. So, you're telling me I have to pre-dig a hole for…things?"

He took a deep breath. "Yes, you need a pre-dug hole, so you aren't digging at night. It gets really dark. It's not like you have to go far into the woods. I'll put the TP by the small table I brought to set up along with the disposable bags we'll throw away in the trash bag later. No big. What were you going to do? Just hold it and explode?"

"If I must," I said a bit too loudly.

He held his hands up. "Everyone pees, Hazel."

"Well, I mean, I know that."

"So?" He shrugged. "Grab the damn shovel."

"Yes, sir, right away, sir. Gonna just go grab the poo shovel and put it by the food, sounds awesome." I stomped off and grabbed the shovel from the back of the Jeep. It was a small, black thing, maybe two feet long, and it looked brand-new. I had this sudden horror that I'd been riding in the Jeep with human feces covering metal just waiting to be looked at.

I put it near the campsite then grabbed the small table and started unloading the food. After I was done doing that, I found a few rocks nearby and made a campfire circle by the tent—not too close since we didn't want to burn down the only shelter we had.

I was actually proud of myself when I finished up. It was already getting pretty dark when I grabbed the firewood and started setting it in the pit.

August came over by me and stared down at my handiwork. "Are you making nature Jenga?"

"Huh?" I looked up. "I read somewhere about making a campfire where you stack it back and forth, then shove the kindling and everything else underneath and blow."

His smile was full-blown beautiful, reaching his eyes in a way that made me look down to not feel its effects. "Well, you have the blow part right."

Before I realized what I was saying, I answered, "I blow just fine, thank you."

"Sure, you do," he said under his breath. "I'll grab the rest of our supplies so we can start dinner. You good with hotdogs and chips?"

I nodded, even though he couldn't fully see me. "Yeah, I'm starving. I'll grab the small grill from the back. Or are you wanting to cook it on one of the griddles?"

He suddenly clapped a hand over my mouth and pulled me against him. "Don't move."

Heart thudding against my chest, I waited for more instructions. Everyone was already in their tents or RVs, and they weren't that close to our campsite. The rustling didn't sound like a large animal, but I was still freaked out.

August pulled me closer against his chest and looked around. Slowly, he tugged his phone out of his pocket and turned on the flashlight, pointing it at the woods.

A small squirrel stared up at us as if we were the crazy ones, but behind the squirrel, a raccoon.

"Shhhh," August whispered in my ear. "I'll scare it away, but you can't be too careful. A lot of them have rabies, and our trash attracts them. We'll have to dig the bathroom closer to camp."

Lovely.

He got up and grabbed a stick from the firepit, then smacked it against a tree. "Hey."

The raccoon scurried off into the woods, but the squirrel stood strong. Ah, brave little one, who would likely steal our food later. We should probably keep all the food in the ice chest and put it away at night in the Jeep.

I made a mental note and looked at the shovel beside the table. "No time better than the present."

August turned around as I saluted him with the shovel. "Where am I digging?"

He grinned. "There."

He pointed at a tree behind the tent. It was maybe six feet away. "And don't forget to bury."

I squeezed my eyes shut. "I can't believe our dads are making us do this."

"They have their reasons," August said quietly. "I'll start dinner."

Chapter Nine

"Always, and I do mean always, bring a shovel." —Hazel Titus

August

She was pretty quiet for having to dig a hole to squat over. I almost got worried when she didn't return for a few minutes, but when she did, she looked like she'd accomplished something. I refused to tell her that she had some dirt on her cheek. I liked the way it dirtied up her pretty skin.

Fixating on her would not make the pain of leaving Mom and Dad go away, nor would it do anything but offer the time I needed for all of us. At least I had Hazel and her many distractions, dirt included.

I smiled down at the ground and rolled the hotdogs around with the tongs. I'd decided to go with the grill since I felt bad about the shovel, and no, I didn't actually make beans; I just wanted to scare her a bit or maybe get a reaction. These last years, helping Dad take care of Mom, giving everything up, knowing what the end result would be, I'd felt so sad, so numb to everything. Watching her every reaction kind of made me feel alive again.

I felt like one of those lame kids in school who picked on their crush just so they could see the emotion, except it was a selfish thing because mine was lacking, and she still didn't know why I'd agreed to the trip. Why I thought it was a good idea for a grown-ass man to go on a let's-make-peace camping trip with the girl next door like he couldn't say no to his parents. Especially when he had his own money, a job fixing motorcycles and classic cars, a life, etcetera. The problem was, my job was only there so I stayed busy. We were Wellingtons. We worked for fun, not because we had to.

I swallowed the lump in my throat when she thrust the shovel into the air. "I did it."

"I dig it," I joked lamely.

She spiked the shovel into the ground by the tent and sat in one of the chairs by the fire. "This is actually nice."

She'd think differently when she had to spend the night in the tent with me. God, I prayed she didn't snore. "You don't happen to have a cold, right?"

She frowned, her brown eyebrows furrowing in the cutest way. "No, why? I mean, I don't think so. I'm feeling good."

"Just checking. It's a scientific fact that bears are attracted to loud noises, and I don't want to get mauled over your mouth-breathing." I grinned. "Hungry?"

She rolled her eyes. "I can't tell if I like you or want to punch you in the face, but yes, thanks for cooking while I dug us a hole. Wait, we aren't sharing the hole, right? I did make two. You're on the right, and I'm the left. I'll dig more in the morning. And why in the hell am I talking about bathrooms in nature while staring at a hotdog?"

I shrugged. "Just one of life's many mysteries."

I handed her one of the paper plates and used the tongs to grab a hotdog for her, placing it on the bun.

She got up and put on an ungodly amount of relish and mustard.

I stared.

Stared harder.

She was going to eat it like that?

"No ketchup?" I pointed at her with the tongs.

She had the hotdog halfway to her mouth and then frowned. "Dude, all you need is mustard and relish. Trust me on this. Great-Grandma passed down the secret."

"I doubt you *and* her." I was still pointing the tongs.

She jumped up with her plate and kneeled in front of me, holding her hotdog up to my lips. "Then take a bite, big guy."

Shit.

Just. Shit.

I had to sleep with her in the same area, and she was holding a hotdog up to my mouth after telling me how good she blew on things.

Should I just walk into the cold ocean now and breathe in saltwater?

"Um…" Damn it. The dirt was still on her cheek.

Look away.

Puppies. Hurricanes. Earthquakes. Aliens. Think of anything but her mouth. Anything.

My lips parted as she shoved the hotdog in. I had to admit, I'd rather eat her, but instead, I was getting schooled in how to doctor up my food.

Frowning, I kept chewing and nodded. "That's good."

She patted me on the head.

She rarely touched me.

I froze.

She froze.

I stopped chewing.

Suddenly, she stood and went back to her chair. "See, I can be right."

"You can." I saluted her. "I bow down to your amazing hotdog recipe. I tragically lack the skill."

"But you did cook." She pointed her hotdog at me. "And they're juicy, really good, nice."

I coughed out a thanks and made my own food. By the time we were done eating, it was time to sleep, and I was forced to put everything away with her in an effort to avoid the smallest tent I'd ever packed in my entire life.

I stared down at it. There was nothing left to do. I stared harder.

She walked up next to me. "Okay, all the food is secure in the cooler inside the Jeep. Here are the keys, just in case." She slammed them into my hand. "And I put some water near the tent in case you wake up and—"

She touched her stomach.

"And?" I prompted.

"Um." Her eyes went wide as she looked behind me, then at the tent, then stared down at the shovel like it was her ending. "Um, I suddenly really have to go to the bathroom. Number one, not number two."

"You're an adult. You can tell me if you need to take a piss, Hazel. Just go around the tent and—" Immediately, a rustling sounded, then I heard what might have been a growl.

She jumped against me, plastering her face to my chest. "It's probably the raccoon again," I said.

"I can't pee with it watching me."

"It has no feelings."

"I do, though." She wrapped her arms around my waist. "Plus, I can't see. How am I going to see?"

"Okay, at the risk of getting too detailed here, do you really need to watch when you wipe, or can you just pop a squat, do a little shake, use a square, toss it into a bag, and move on your merry way?"

"I'm not a boy. I don't have a dick that I can just shake in the wind."

"Right," I said slowly as I hugged her. "Because that is exactly what we do. We face the wind and shake—not too hard, though, because that's something else completely."

She elbowed me in the ribs. "I'm serious. What do I do?"

"You pee proudly—into the wind, apparently."

"Be serious."

"Hazel, do you want me to take you to the hole?"

She squirmed against my chest. "You'll close your eyes?"

"I don't need that kind of free show, Hazel."

She moaned and then pulled back, taking a deep breath. "I drank a lot of water."

"As humans should."

"And I just need to get rid of it."

"So you don't die. Yes, human nature, I encourage that." I was nearly shaking from trying not to laugh at her. "Let's walk behind the tent. I'll hold the flashlight and look the other way, I'll even hum for you while you pee. Just promise me you make it in the hole, okay?"

She nodded. "Fine, yes, thank you. Okay, I'm sorry."

"For going to the bathroom?" I grabbed her hand and reached for the flashlight, not even really thinking because it felt natural to guide her to our makeshift outhouse. I didn't have time to overanalyze too much as we grabbed a bag, the TP, and the shovel and went to the back of the tent and our bathroom area.

"Nice holes." I nodded.

"Not the time," she snapped.

I grinned and handed her a bag. "Sorry, I always feel like compliments make people more at ease."

Her glare said otherwise.

"Okay, then." I guided her toward the hole, turned on my flashlight, and pointed it at her, then turned around. "Good luck."

"Good luck?" Did she call me an idiot after that? Or was it the wind? "I'm just going to squat like it's a workout I hate and go."

"Yup."

"Good."

"Perfect." I stared out at the ocean. "At least, it's loud."

"I can't," she whimpered a minute later. "I can't."

"Can't squat?"

"I can't pee. It's stuck."

My heavy sigh probably didn't help. "Okay, just take a deep breath and release."

"A deep breath and release? Release what? The Kraken? I can't just release."

"Stop panicking!" I didn't mean to yell. "Sorry. Just a few deep breaths, count to ten." I shivered; it really was getting cold. "And exhale."

"Okay."

"One."

"Didn't need you to actually do it out loud."

"I misunderstood."

I tried not to laugh and had to bite my bottom lip. "Okay, just count to three, then inhale, count to six, exhale, and free the water."

"Not water," she huffed. "I mean, it was water. It is. Son of a bitch. Why is this so hard?"

I sighed and started mumbling, "Row, row, row your boat—"

"That is in no way helpful."

I paused then. "Gently down the stream."

"Merrily," she joined in, "merrily, merrily, life is but a dream." We finished in sync.

I cleared my throat. "The harmony could use some work."

"I was under duress," she snapped. "Okay, done. I'm done. Thank you. I'm sorry, this is just…like what is it, even? Never mind. I'm grabbing the shovel."

"And that, kids…" I still hadn't turned around. "…is how I met your mother."

"Pardon?"

"It was a joke."

"Hear the laughter?"

Crickets, all I heard was crickets—both figuratively and literally. "I'm going to have to say no."

The sound of shoveling filled the air. "Okay. I think I put enough sand on it."

I looked over my shoulder. It took an insurmountable level of self-control not to laugh. "So, you made a shrine?"

She pointed with the shovel in the cutest way possible at the giant mound of sand piled higher than the Sahara after a storm. "I wanted to make sure."

"That your pee was worshiped? Because I gotta say, nobody is going to miss this, bears included. You may as well have put a sign on the sand that said: *I peed here, honor me.* Somewhere in there, I feel like there could be a very strategic OnlyFans account. I mean, if a girl can sell her farts, think of the possibilities."

"Shut up." Her smile was everything; it spread wide and free across her face. I took the shovel and poked it into the ground.

"I'm proud," she said.

"That you were able to go to the bathroom?"

"No, that I dug a hole, crouched without pulling a muscle, and didn't die of embarrassment, all within five minutes."

I frowned. "Why be embarrassed? It's just me."

Her gaze flickered away from mine. Finding something interesting on the sand, maybe? "I know, it's just…peeing in a hole isn't like…attractive. And I think I've spent my whole life being that person, the one everyone thinks is too tall, too gangly, too different. It doesn't help that I prefer books to people, but—"

"Stop." I leaned down and touched her right shoulder. My fingers met warm skin, even through her sweatshirt. "You're beautiful, and anyone who tells you differently is both an idiot and an asshole we should feed to that rabid raccoon we met earlier, all right?"

Her head slowly lifted, and her eyes met mine.

Hazel's parted lips were a temptation I couldn't afford. They beckoned, made me want to brush my thumb across them, and tell her just how stunning she really was. But the words died in my throat. I shouldn't. I couldn't. I wasn't even sorry for all the above reasons. I'd be messing with her emotions, and she'd be leaving anyway. What good was it to tell her I was attracted to her or that she had way more value than she could ever possibly know? Hell, half my friends had been in love with her in high school. It was the girls who had been the issue, the jealousy, the constant putting her down. And it didn't help that my popularity had been more important to me than almost anything at the time. Before Mom got sick, I'd been such a selfish prick. I didn't blame Hazel for hating me; I would have hated me, too.

There were so many conversations and words that should have taken place with that girl and her parted lips and large brown eyes, but I'd buried them. Ha. Ironic since we'd just done that, and I had a shovel by my foot.

"I, um..." She pointed behind her. "I should go get some hand sanitizer and clean up the campsite before it starts raining harder."

"Yeah." I nodded. "Last thing we need is for you to get wet."

She tripped over a rock and almost faceplanted into the tent.

"You okay?" I reached for her, but she was already up dusting the sand from her leggings.

"Totally!"

"Why are you yelling?"

"Rain. The rain." She sniffled. There was no thunder, no lightning, only a light drizzle that wasn't at all loud. "It threw me off."

I nodded slowly. "Yes, I can see how the storm could do that to a person."

"Right?" She moved around the campsite, organizing the rest of our belongings while I stoked the fire and went into the Jeep to grab some extra blankets.

Damn. It was going to be tight in that little tent, and it was starting to rain harder. Maybe staying in the vehicle would be smarter, but it would be so uncomfortable and not warm at all. Besides, I could stoke the fire a bit longer and we could feed off that heat.

"All right." I cleared my throat and awkwardly pointed at the tent with both hands as if to say, *"Your honeymoon suite awaits."*

All I needed was a tux and a rose dangling out of my mouth like an idiot. And why the hell was I still pointing with both hands? Where did I even put my hands? In my pockets? I imagined if you were watching me on TV, you'd be like...that poor, pathetic bastard.

"Yeah." She bit her lower lip again. Stop it, damn it. Stop it. Stop it right now. "I'll just follow your lead."

Why did she use those words? Why, God? Why?

"Sure," I agreed. "I'm just going to kick off my shoes and hop in. The fire should be good for the next hour or so, but I'll check on it if it really starts to get cold. Though the rain might end up putting out." Her eyes widened. "Putting *it* out. I meant putting it out."

"Oh, I know," she said quickly. "Because it's wet."

Has there ever been a more awkward campfire moment? Tough to say, honestly, tough to say. There was that one time I ran around in my underwear when I was ten and hit a tree.

Pretty sure I would claim that over this moment any day.

Becoming one with bark.

"So..." I gulped. Why was I suddenly so awkward? "I'll just get in there."

God, please, someone tell me to stop talking. Why did everything feel like a sexual innuendo?

"I'm ready," she answered brightly.

Maybe next time, we'd just use hand signals and save ourselves from the awkward misery of our own inability to speak.

"Yup." Just going in. I crept inside the small tent and kicked off my boots, putting them right outside in case I needed to tend to the fire or go to my hole, which sounded off even in my brain.

She sat down just inside and took off her tennis shoes, setting them next to my boots, then scooted in, socks still on. I had the extra blankets on her side, the one pillow in the middle, and the sleeping bag open. It would be impossible to zip it, so we'd just have to pile on the blankets and lie down.

Together.

We had maybe three feet across at best and around eight feet to stretch out in.

I used the flashlight and quickly zipped up the tent right when the rain started to pour onto us so loudly that it made Hazel jump closer to me and grab on. "Downpour?"

"It's not going to hit us super hard since we're under the tree."

"Okay." She looked down and pulled her hands free from my sweatshirt. "Sorry. I didn't realize, and it's hard to see."

"It's okay," I rasped. "Just try to get some sleep. Can you toss me one of the blankets or two? I'll pull them over us."

"Yeah." She grabbed both down blankets and abruptly turned toward me, nailing me in the head with her chin. "Ouch!"

"Wow." I stretched my face. "Strong chin."

"It's dark."

"It's the mountains." I rubbed the side of my head and pulled the blankets over us, then reclined on the pillow. She slowly stretched out next to me.

I put the flashlight between us, casting a glow on her face. "You know something?"

"What?" She tucked her hands under her head.

I didn't touch her, but I wanted to. "You're pretty."

Her eyes widened, but I chose to turn off the light, just like I turned off all temptation.

I wasn't sure how much more space my heart could make for someone in this world, knowing that they could be taken, too. It wasn't something people really thought about until they were faced with it.

Loss.

You can't just replace what's been lost. You can make room for more, but why take that risk? And I genuinely—despite what almost everyone thought—liked Hazel.

She'd probably marry a rock star or something.

Someone totally against the grain.

I smiled to myself as she started to snore softly next to me. Yeah, she'd be the pain in the ass who brought home a guy with long hair and an obsession with guitars, drumsticks, and weed.

I almost burst out laughing. Her dad would shit a brick.

My smile fell as my brain continued stupidly functioning in that little scenario: her getting married and taking pictures by her tree.

Maybe wearing something from her great-grandma.

And me, alone, next door, while Dad traveled to keep himself busy.

Me in an empty house, keeping my grief at bay.

Me fixing a motorcycle and finally finishing college, going to a boring job, just because that's what you did.

Dating but not feeling it.

But why wouldn't I?

I liked sex.

I liked women.

I liked the thrill of it all. So when did I lose interest in all of that, and why was picturing Hazel getting married and moving on with her life as she should so depressing?

In an effort to get close to her, I'd made fun of her once. And then it was just…gone. I graduated, she stayed, then *I* stayed, and she left for college. Why would that even matter?

"I want that for you," Mom had said when I was in high school.

"What?" I looked next door where she pointed.

Sure enough, Great-Grandma Nadine was sneaking out of the house, cane and all, and walking down the street toward her lover's house. And just like clockwork, Mr. Casbon looked out his blinds like a peeping Tom and hurriedly opened the door as he escorted her in.

She was carrying a bottle of wine.

And he was wearing one of his notorious Hawaiian shirts.

One time, I'd asked him if he'd ever been, and he just laughed and said he experienced it through his lover.

Aka, Great-Grandma Nadine.

Another time, I asked him where he kept buying them, and he said she bought them for him when she went or when she shopped because each and every one meant she was thinking of him. It was all the vacation he needed.

"Yeah," I'd said to Mom. "They're sneaking around like teenagers."

"It's fun," she said. "Fun. Relationships should be fun."

I didn't get it at the time, but maybe now that's what I got. A girl with a shovel, a giant hill, snoring, and awkward pranks.

Love maybe shouldn't be safe but a hazard to your health.

I flipped back over. Though I didn't need a flashlight to see her shine, even though it was pitch-black.

I pressed my palm to her cheek and fell asleep.

Chapter Ten

"Mornings tend to be awkward after you spoon and then somehow manage to get naked to share body heat. There is no other reason other than heat. Heat. Heat. Heat. Swear. It's only heat."—Hazel Titus

Hazel

It was warm, so very warm. I was suddenly pumped I hadn't brought a tent because this one was amazing. There was no need for me to be upset about the fact that I'd forgotten—

My eyes suddenly blinked open, and I stared down at the blanket I was clutching. Not a blanket, not a blanket.

No, that would be a sweatshirt that belonged to an arm, and that nice, warm, comfy feeling would be the person attached to all the things pressing close against me.

I should pry free, but I was freezing.

And he was so warm.

His face rested right above my boob, and one arm was on my waist—the same one I'd been holding like a blanket—while the other was wrapped around my head.

It was nice.

So nice that I almost imagined this was a normal scenario, us just sleeping in a bright yellow tent, spooning, heating each other up.

I closed my eyes when he moved against me. Oh, wait, he was getting closer. August jerked me against his chest and rolled onto his back, taking me on the journey with him.

Suddenly, I was half on his body.

And he was moaning against my neck.

I froze.

He kept moaning.

The tent moved with our bodies.

"Nice," he whispered in a sleepy, raspy voice. "You feel so nice."

Me? Or was he dreaming about somebody else?

"Hazel," he groaned. "So warm."

And leaning toward getting very, very hot.

He pressed a hand to my hip and squeezed. "Mmmm, so nice."

I opened my mouth to say something when that same hand dipped into my jeans and touched my bare hip.

Oh, shoot. Yeah, that felt nice, warm. His fingertips slid down farther and kept going until he was cupping my ass. I moved against him just a bit, and then I was fully on top of him as he rubbed slow circles on my skin. His erection pressed against my stomach, warm and solid, like steel you actually wanted to wrap your hands around and squeeze.

I let out a loud exhale when he rolled his hips.

This was bad, so bad. Should I wake him up? Pretend to be sleeping and slap him in the face?

All options were bad, and then nature, or the universe, quite literally provided as the sound of a wild animal filled the air.

August jolted awake, nearly headbutting me, and sat up while I tumbled backward. "Was that a bear?"

I stared down at his lap.

His eyes followed my gaze. "Morning."

"I'll say."

"What was that?" He grabbed a blanket.

"It's a great morning. So many reasons to be perky and ready for the day." I laughed and looked away while he grabbed our solo pillow and slammed it against me. "What?"

"Very funny. How'd you sleep?" He yawned, stretching his arms over his head. "Good, I hope."

"Probably not as well as you," I joked, earning another slight pillow slam before he actually reached for me and tugged me back down against him. I didn't resist.

"Don't." He held me close. "Don't make this weird. We never talk about this, but that was the best sleep I've had in a really long time. Can we please have a few more minutes before things get all chaotic again and you build more shrines?"

"Sure." I smiled to myself and yawned, then turned into his chest. "But just like five minutes."

"Just five," he agreed.

Two hours later, we both jolted awake at the sound of rustling.

August rubbed his eyes. "How did we sleep so long?"

I shook my head. "No clue, but I keep hearing noises, and it's not your snoring."

He gave me a slight shove. "Yeah, okay, one who purrs at night. Don't think I didn't hear you wake yourself up at least three times from your own noises."

"I was scared."

"So your throat just automatically went—?" He started making snoring noises while I shoved him to the ground, laughing, only to hear another rustle outside the tent. "What is that, you think?"

"A bunny, a deer? Not a bear. Maybe a fly got super aggressive. Who knows?"

I rolled my eyes. "Fine, fine. Let's forage for our breakfast. And when I say forage, I mean you cook, and I'll go find more kindling."

"Deal." He held up his hand for a high five. "I brought sausage."

We both paused.

Do not look down, do not look down.

He winced. "So many words that should not be shared or said. So many jokes, too. It's almost painful."

"I'm sure something is," I said sweetly and then, in a moment of pure insanity, ran my hand down his shirt and paused at the waistband of his jeans. Then, I pulled away. "I'll be back with that wood…" I grinned. "And kindling."

"Tease," he yelled. "That's mean. I'm not that strong."

"You'll survive. It's nature."

"You'll survive!" he yelled back.

"Dude, that was your comeback?"

"Oh, I'm sorry." August threw up his hands. His hair was all over the place, and his face was full of what seemed to be terminal frustration. "I'm sorry I'm horny as fuck and was forced to sleep next to this gorgeous human I've crushed on for years while living emotional trauma in my dreams."

I paused. "What did you just say?"

He frowned. "Nothing. I was thinking."

"Yeah, you said all of that out loud."

"When?"

"Just now."

"Right now?"

"Yeah, like seconds ago. I'll wait for it to sink in. You're really one of those people, aren't you? I almost didn't believe it, but now I do. You have no censor and forget that words actually come out of the mouth and don't always stay between the ears."

He jumped to his feet, nearly knocking over the tent, then stomped out. "I'll just go see a bear about that firewood."

"You do that," I called, then grabbed my shoes. "Just be safe. Remember, act big when you're small."

"I *am* big," he snapped.

I held up my hands and followed him out of the tent, still laughing, though the laughter was short-lived once we were five minutes into our walk for kindling.

"August," I hissed. "Don't move."

I saw everything before he did. He was clearly still delirious from waking up with a boner and had zero brain cells left. I was still triumphantly telling myself it was because I caused it, made him dizzy with thoughts and confessions. I should hate him, but in those moments, I kind of wanted to throw myself all over him and make him crazy again just to see what he'd say.

August held up his hands without looking back at me. "Why am I not moving? If this is your weird idea of freeze tag, I'm not a fan. I'm too hungry, tired, horny—and yes, I said horny, so get over it—to deal with a prank right now."

"It's at the campsite behind us. I think it's a bear, or maybe that raccoon again. It's hard to tell from here with the tree branches blocking a lot of my view."

"Is it white? Brown? Black? Does it climb? Is it a matter of life or death? Is it eating my chocolate? Because I swear if those Hersheys get stolen, I will lose my shit."

"It's not eating your chocolate; it's chewing on those tongs we used to move the hotdogs around."

He exhaled. "My fault. I should have put them away."

"Either way, it's not looking like a grizzly," I said as the animal wandered off.

"He'll be back." He slowly looked over his shoulder, hands still up like we were in a holdup. "He'll be back for sure after tasting that wiener."

I stared.

August stared right back.

I stared harder.

He sighed. "It's still early. My brain isn't functioning."

"I kind of like not-functioning August." I winked. "And I think it's a she."

"How so?"

"Safe to say, the tree branches are no longer an issue, and she's huge. Like she's carrying her young."

"Shh, quiet. It could spur her to turn back and chew on things, mainly us. Us equals things."

"Well, she took our shelter, and we're seconds away from climbing up into our own tree right now. So, I'm sorry for panicking about the thief."

The sound of wolves howling filled the air. August cursed under his breath. "Yeah, well, that checks out, doesn't it? Why not add wolves to the mix of hell from nature?"

"Shh." I clapped a hand over his mouth. "They'll hear you. And I can't run faster than you."

August slammed my hand away. "That was actually an option for you? Letting me die?"

I winced. "I mean, as long as it's not me."

"You're impossible."

"And you're just—" My mouth dropped open. "Don't move."

He froze. "Those are not safe words in a safe sentence."

"Just…" My eyes were wide as I took in the situation. "It's not a big deal, just stay very still while I think."

"Think about what? What thoughts? What's going on?" he hissed between his teeth. "Hazel?"

"It's going to be fine." I said it like it was true while panic ensued.

Chapter Eleven

"When all else fails, pivot."—Hazel Titus

August

"Are you allergic to any sort of insect?" Hazel asked slowly as she pulled her hand away from the tree and stared me down. "You know, like murder hornets or something crazy like that?"

"Those exist?" I asked, my voice cracking while still looking behind her and wondering if I had to find a machete because of the bear or just roll around in the sand to repel insects.

"No. I mean, yes, but we don't have any here right now. It was just a general question after the whole don't-move thing."

"Bees." My dark, hushed tone wasn't making me feel better. If anything, it was like I already knew. "I'm allergic to bees, the honey ones."

"Oh." She perked up like she'd just gotten a shot of adrenaline and clapped her hands in front of her. "Good. Because I think it's just a really big hornets' nest, but it's scary close to your head, and they just started moving a lot. I think if we move a lot with them, then they'll move more, so maybe we very slowly climb up past them. Or just take our chances with the bear."

"How many hornets?" I ground my teeth.

"A lot." The buzzing picked up near my right ear. I nodded and slowly started moving toward her. The tree bark was rough against my palm. We could easily go up past the hornets' nest and wait for the bear to leave, or we could just make a run for it toward the water and hope it would scare the bear and not make him or her chase us.

I held out my hand. "I think we flee the crime scene and forget about our healthy foraging and firewood."

She reached for me but stared behind me at the hornets' nest as rustling sounded behind her. "Oh, crap."

I tugged her next to me, and we started running back around the campsite and onto the beach, only to see the bear blocking the path we needed to take.

"Yup, that is definitely a bear," she shrieked while the small brown bear looked at us, then continued rummaging through our tent. "Back away. Slowly."

"The Jeep," I said through clenched teeth. "Back slowly away and get in the Jeep."

"Keys?"

"Unlocked," I whispered. "In three, two, one." We both scrambled into the back seat while I threw my body over and locked the doors.

The bear didn't even seem to care.

"He's so tame," Hazel whispered, only to have the bear stand up on his legs and roar into the sky. "Kidding. I offended him. Sorry, bear. He's terrifying. He's going to kill us. We're going to die in here, aren't we?"

I pulled her against me. "No, he'll get tired. Smell more food. We just have to hold out longer than the bear."

Her stomach rumbled.

Mine followed suit.

I let out a sigh and nodded toward the blue ice chest still in the back. "At least we have some food and water. We just can't go to our holes."

"Holes?" she repeated. "Ohhhh, the holes."

"Hey, maybe we'll get lucky, and he'll find your giant mound of sand and get distracted enough for us to gather our things, find a hotel, lie to our dads, and tell them camping went great."

Her laughter was all I needed. It filled the Jeep in a big way—a way that had me genuinely smiling.

And then she frowned. "You have your phone? Keys and wallet?"

Where was she going with that? "I have my phone and my wallet, but the keys are at the campsite in my jeans."

She nodded slowly, her eyes taking in the tent. "How much does a tent like that cost?"

"Huh?"

"How much?" She smacked me on the shoulder. "Just answer the question."

"Ouch!" I rubbed the spot and then shoved her head down while the bear looked over at us. "I don't know. Like maybe eighty bucks?"

"And your clothes in that duffel bag over there?" She pointed. "The chairs?"

I threw up a hand. "I mean, not a lot. I didn't bring a ton, and the chairs are old. Why are you asking about how much shit costs?"

"My purse is in here," she said. "We basically have everything we need and can come back tomorrow, pack up the campsite, and make the dads think we stayed one more night. If the campsite gets semi-destroyed, then we'll just be honest. A bear attacked us because of our musk."

"Musk? Because of our musk?"

"Yeah." She was adorable with her dirty blond hair pulled back into a sad, traumatized ponytail. "We must have attracted it. You know, through hormones or something."

"First musk and now hormones? I'm sorry, but are you having a moment? Why would a bear be attracted to our musk? Now, the little hole you dug? Possibly. But musk? Nah, it probably wanted our food, and we're in its territory."

"Hormones, then." She nodded with such finality that even I was almost convinced. "It could smell the estrogen."

"Not the testosterone?"

"Meh." She waved me off. "Probably not strong enough. You'd have to be super horny, and I doubt bears do it for you."

Immediately uncomfortable in my jeans, I cleared my throat. "Yeah, solid scientific point, because…science. And bears." Why was I laughing like a maniac? I nervously tugged at my sweatshirt. "Anyway, let's just find a way to grab the keys. We'll drive to a nearby hotel, then come back and rescue what we can before going home. Nobody has to know."

"Nobody has to know." She nodded. "Okay. So you said the keys are in your jeans from last night?"

I nodded. "Yup. Back pocket."

Hazel looked down at the jeans I was wearing, then back up at me. "You changed in the tent last night?"

Goose bumps erupted down my arms. "They were uncomfortable, so I just wiggled"—poor choice of words—"into a new pair. So, yes, I changed in the tent. It's not like you saw anything, peeping Tom. You were snoring mid-change."

"You were naked. And I do not snore."

"You probably attracted the bear even more," I pointed out. "Now, let's focus on what's important: grabbing the keys and escaping. I say you provide a distraction. You know, make your body really big, get his attention. I'll sprint to the tent, grab the jeans, and run back. By then, he'll only be semi-hostile, and we can start the Jeep."

Hazel frowned over at me and crossed her arms. "So I'm bait?"

"But..." I leaned in and patted her on the knee. "Very nice bait. Attractive bait. Do you think the bear's attracted to a person like me?" I made a face. "Gross, no, never. But you? Tall, beautiful, bold, and strong, almost like you were born to play the Disney princess from *Brave*. That will throw him for a loop."

She was silent and then said, "I can't decide what's sadder, the fact that the bear would somehow recognize a Disney movie or character or that I think you actually believe the bullshit that's coming out of your mouth. Bait, just say it. I'm bait, and you're the runner."

I gripped her by the shoulders. "Brother Bear could turn on me, too, you know."

"Hated that movie," she grumbled.

"So sad, right?" I agreed.

"And with the Northern Lights." She sighed. "Never mind, we're getting distracted because we're nervous to face a bear that probably weighs more than your car."

I nodded. "All true."

"Okay." She took three deep breaths. I ignored how it brought attention to her tight, black sweatshirt. "Okay," she said again. "Here's what we do. You sprint first and try not to get noticed. The minute you do, I'll jump out of the car and redirect while you jump in and start the engine. Then I'll jump in after you, and we can take off."

"Foolproof," I lied. "Totally foolproof. Plus, the bear already ate a ton of food. How hungry can he be for human flesh?"

A loud scraping echoed through the Jeep. Slowly, we both turned and gaped as the cute brown bear started scratching, raking its claws down the bark of the nearest tree.

Hazel gripped my hand and squeezed. "Be honest. Do you do coke?"

"What the hell, Hazel? No."

"It's a valid question."

"How the hell is that a valid question?"

"*Cocaine Bear*!" she shouted. "The movie. Where these drug smugglers leave cocaine behind, and the bear goes on this binge, and—?"

"How the ever-loving shit did we go from *Brother Bear* to *Cocaine Bear*?"

"Life." She made it sound like she had sage advice to follow. "I mean, he looks like he just went on a binge. He went from looking like a bear that would share porridge and dreams to one who would slit you from your toes all the way up to your spleen."

"Graphic."

"I tried to tame it down."

"I can tell."

She took a deep breath. "Okay, just go slow and then sprint."

I frowned over at her. "In what universe do the words leaving your mouth sound like advice that makes sense?"

"Logic!" Both her fists smacked my chest. "You've got this. Valhalla."

Okay, she was adorable. "You just said *Valhalla* like I was a Viking going out to war."

She tucked her head against my chest, probably not realizing she was doing it, and laughed, then pulled back while I grabbed her by the wrists and tugged her closer against me. "It seemed like the most encouraging thing to say. Plus, Uhtred says it, and he's never wrong."

"Uhtred," I said in my best accent. "Son of Uhtred."

"He's pretty." She licked her lips and pressed her palms against my chest, sliding them up slowly. "Just saying."

"Maybe I'll be pretty, too, if I chant that when facing the bear."

She swallowed, her eyes locking onto my mouth before pulling away. I didn't want to lose her heat, so I didn't let her move. Instead, I pressed her against the door, then placed my hands on either side of her. "What are you doing?"

"Oh, I thought this was part of screaming *Valhalla*. Never know when you'll see me again, fair maiden. Better give me my kiss."

"Better ask permission, Berserker."

I couldn't stop smiling. "Care to inspire me?"

"But you hate me."

"Hate is such a strong word," I confessed. "It's easier to use hate to mask other emotions, don't you think?"

Hazel let out a rough exhale, and her chest rose and fell hard and fast. "What do you mean?"

"You're damaging to my soul, Hazel Titus," I whispered against her neck. "Now, wish me luck before I go face a bear next to your shrine and our yellow tent."

She giggled, and the movement caused her body to rise just enough that my mouth caught on her warm neck again. I breathed in her scent, counted her heartbeats, and then pulled away.

I'd never leave the Jeep if something started, and our parents would find us wondering how the hell we lost track of time, food, water, and sanity.

But that was Hazel.

She was damaging to my mental and physical health, and the longer we spent with each other, the more I realized that this was the reason I'd pushed her away so much to begin with. Because what if?

I hated that phrase.

What if I dated her?

What if she liked me back?

And what if I lost her?

It was the most immature and selfish thought, but I knew I couldn't be that guy. The person who just jumped in headfirst and prayed it would be okay. I wasn't that trusting of her or myself, not to mention the universe.

I sobered and pulled back.

"Um…" I scratched my head. "The minute the bear sees me and starts getting angry, just try to be a distraction. I'm only a few feet away."

"And you did run track," she pointed out.

I saluted her. "Kind of you to remind me of my second-place state trophy."

"Sucks that second isn't first, huh?"

I smacked her lightly on the thigh. "You never quit, do you?"

"Admit it." She leaned in. "You don't want me to."

Shit.

All I saw were her light pink lips.

And the fog filling up our side of the Jeep.

Fifty-fifty.

We'd end up together, fighting until death did us part, or we'd damage each other beyond repair.

I jerked away from her and reached for the door. "Keep a lookout for the Bernstein Bear."

"Berenstain," she corrected.

"Yeah, okay, time shifter," I hissed and opened the door slowly, then made a run for it.

The bear didn't even budge. It just kept scratching the tree as I went to the tent and grabbed my jeans. I even had time to get the keys out.

Hazel lifted her arms in confusion from the back seat. I shrugged as if to say, *"Yeah, no clue how we got away with that."*

Grin smug, I was maybe a foot from the Jeep when I heard a crack and looked down.

A branch.

A branch under my foot.

Slowly, I looked over my right shoulder.

Hell was waiting for me there.

With a yell, I grabbed the driver's side door and jerked it open, then started the Jeep and hit the accelerator with a bear close behind me.

"Ahhhhh!" Hazel screamed as she got thrown across the back seat. "I'm not buckled in."

"But you are alive." I took a turn, then another, then went up onto the highway and headed toward the small town of Canon Beach. "You're alive."

I was damn near hyperventilating when she crawled into the front seat, buckled up, and turned to me, her brown eyes twinkling. "*Naked and Afraid* has nothing on us."

"Well," I joked, "at least the afraid part. We didn't have to get naked."

The air thickened.

Shit.

Again, I did it to myself.

"I guess." Her voice was quiet. "There are no rules in nature, anyway."

Vague.

I wanted to ask her what she meant, and then I wanted to analyze and digest every part of the sentence.

My grip tightened on the steering wheel. "We'll just find a hotel."

Yes, because that would fix every ounce of sexual tension—forced proximity, a comfy bed, bathrobes, and adrenaline.

Sure.

Oh, the lies we tell ourselves.

Chapter Twelve

"When you're a hot mess, the best choice is to just own it and jump in with both feet, then succumb to the hotness before you explode."—Hazel Titus

Hazel

We stopped at the first hotel we could find that was right on the beach, far, far away from the bear.

They had several rooms.

Which made it awkward. Did we pay for two?

I was about to ask for two when August requested a King corner suite, then ordered wine and food.

No complaints.

It was easy to check into the hotel. We used the secret credit card Great-Grandma had gotten for me so that neither of our dads could trace anything—not that either of them really had access, but we didn't want to take any chances.

Parents had their ways.

We were at a small resort called Salty Peak. It had maybe forty rooms tops and was newer. They even had bikes you could rent, a gorgeous spa, and from what I'd seen, the rooms would be new and modern.

August was quiet on the elevator ride up, and when he tapped the card against the door and opened it, I almost wept.

The suite was at least nine hundred square feet done up in blacks and whites with bold turquoise accent pillows and art. It had a huge balcony to the right, and a small one to the left, with a fireplace in the middle.

The bathroom was huge with its white marble and glass shower, which kind of meant that he'd have to look away unless he wanted to see me naked.

"So…" I turned in a small circle and dropped into one of the chairs when a knock sounded at the door. I moved to get up, but August was already there.

Room service sure was fast.

He thanked the guy and rolled the cart into the room. Cheese, grapes, two bottles of red wine, crackers, and two yummy-looking dips greeted us.

I reached for a cracker. "This is how the trip should have started."

He grunted. "Next time, we just bring the tent inside the hotel room and say, yes, we camped."

I almost choked on my cracker. "Next time?"

"Yeah, I figure we need a re-do." He licked his lips and uncorked the wine, pouring each of us a glass. "Since the parents will never stop until we get along, and since I never really want to get along with you, this might be a yearly thing."

I actually did choke on my cracker this time, then grabbed my glass of wine and took a few sips. "What do you mean, you don't want to get along with me? That's really mean. What did I ever do to you that would make you want to fight with me all the time?"

"Fighting makes me feel alive," he said. "And sometimes you need to feel alive. I figure if I can just fight with you for the rest of my life, then I'll at least get some parts of you. Maybe that's selfish, but I can at least have one small part, right?"

I couldn't tell if he was joking. He had a small, sad smile on his face as if I were somehow leaving him or he was leaving me.

I was too tired to really read the room. All I felt was this tension between us and words that maybe were spoken but not really leaned into.

I took another brave sip of wine. "We don't always have to fight."

"Fighting's healthy." He looked away and set his wineglass down. "Do you want to watch a movie or something? Just relax and hang out for a bit?"

"Yeah, sure." Special moment gone, we took our snacks and wine to the bed and sat next to each other.

He put on *Happy Gilmore*. Classic. We didn't talk much, which I hated because I'd kind of been enjoying his company up until now, something I would take to my grave.

The next movie started playing.

And I almost dropped my wineglass. It was *Unfaithful*, where this married woman has an affair with one of the hottest men alive. While it starts out pretty normal, I knew it got really hot and heavy.

But I didn't want to be the person to switch the channel.

And he didn't seem to want to be that person either.

Neither of us wanted to be the uncomfortable prude.

So, we sat there and took sip after sip.

We watched.

In one scene, the actor reached down the heroine's pants. I squirmed a bit and coughed while the actor's tongue ran down her neck.

Hot, was it hot in here?

No, but it was painful, and all the wine was gone. Had we seriously pounded two bottles? I mean, over the course of a few hours, but still.

The credits started.

It was after noon.

And still we sat, wordless, watching the TV as it turned to something else. He shifted in his spot and set down his wineglass again. "This is bullshit."

"The movies?"

"No, the fact that a bear freaking ruined what could have been a day at the beach. Now, I'm sitting in a stupid hotel room, on a stupid comfortable bed that has no business being this comfortable, with a hot girl I've already kissed and would kiss again, all because our dads are psychopaths and because I was doing mine a favor by giving him the time I knew he needed, using you as an excuse to—"

He stopped talking.

I tilted my head. "An excuse?"

He scowled. "She's sick, Hazel. My mom's sick, and Dad just got home from his last trip. She's not doing better, and he wanted some alone time. Yes, the prank war was probably part of it, but it was just an easy excuse for me to give him some time."

"Excuse?" I repeated. "So, all of this was just me being a reason for you to get away? I mean, I get that you didn't want to spend time with me, but being someone you loathe on top of being an excuse now just makes me feel like baggage."

"Don't make it about you," he snapped, then ran his hands down his face. "I'm sorry, it's not that, it's just…"

"What? What is it, August? Just be truthful."

He was deathly quiet, not making eye contact when he said the words. "You aren't the excuse. I make excuses or *made* excuses to see you. You aren't the excuse, you're the reason. And life hasn't exactly been normal for us. With my mom being sick, I'm taking care of her. I didn't even get to finish my first year of college, and here you are, all smart, brilliant, pretty, and thinking that after six years, I'm still the same person who taunted you from next door. And maybe that's true. Because I do like taunting you. I like teasing you. I like getting a rise out of you because it's cute, you're cute, and I had a crush on you back then. Now, I'm literally having the hardest time sitting a few feet from you on a bed without thinking about what it would be like to taste you again."

My heart stalled in my chest, then got caught in my throat.

The buzz from the TV and the A/C were the only noises in the room.

My exhale shuddered past my lips. I turned to look at him. His hair was a wreck, and he was staring down.

"So, are you done?" I asked.

His head popped up. "What?"

"With your speech. Are you done?"

His eyes moved back and forth, searching mine. "What the hell are you talking about—?"

I jumped onto his lap and straddled him, my legs resting on both sides of his.

His hands gripped my hips as he rolled his beneath me. "Yes, done. I'm totally done. I'll never speak again."

Our mouths collided in a rush, and his hands dove into my hair. Our lips were so meant to meet over and over again, the way his tongue flicked against mine as he moved beneath me.

August was mine.

That was the only sentence that kept repeating itself over and over in my head. That he was mine, and that this was inevitable.

He'd been my best enemy.

My first crush.

And now, I was kissing him.

His hands slid down my neck and then grasped my shoulders before our mouths broke apart in a pant. He nipped at my lip once, twice, three times, then flipped me over onto my back. "Ceasefire," he whispered against my lips.

I could barely breathe; my heart was beating so fast. "Ceasefire? And what happens after?"

Something beautiful broke in his eyes as he stared me down and shook his head. "I don't know anymore. I don't know."

"Tell me the truth," I whispered. "Are you okay?"

I could see the strain in his face. "I don't think so. No."

I rubbed both hands down his back. "Well, I guess it's a good thing we aren't getting attacked by a bear, it gives me the opportunity to be the one attacking."

Tears filled his green eyes. "I don't know if I'm ever going to be whole, Hazel."

I leaned up and kissed his jaw, then found his lips before pulling away. "Don't be stupid, August. You were never supposed to be whole to begin with. When you really think about it, how can you share your soul with someone who has no space left? It's all about the fractured pieces and the people in your life that fill them—so beautiful and ugly at the same time. You have damage? Missing pieces? Wounds? Scars? That's why people are brought into your life. It may not be pretty, but what a beautiful mess in the end, don't you think? All the colors? The personalities? The disasters? I'm sure I have a spot in some of those cracks, some of those missing pieces. Think of it as an honor when people stand by your side, rather than find you lacking in any way."

A tear slid down his cheek and dropped onto his chest. "Who made you so wise?"

I proudly stared him down and whispered, "My great-grandma. Warriors stick together, you know. Plus"—I turned my right hand over and showed him my wrist, where I had a small heart tattoo—"Great-Grandma Nadine Lainheart is infused in me. So, when her soul left, I kept her memories and wisdom and put them in a small tattoo so that no matter what I touched or did with my hands, I'd be reminded of how powerful my words are. How powerful a helping hand can be."

"Did that extend to me?" He brushed his thumb over the heart tattoo.

"Oh, no. I hated you. But she did give me one piece of advice about the boy next door."

"Oh, yeah?" he asked. "What was that?"

"We fight what we love the most because we're afraid if we don't fight for it, we won't actually deserve it in the end."

"Maybe." He swiped his thumb across my lower lip. "We'll never deserve those precious things. Maybe the point is to try to earn them every day."

"One hole and bear at a time," I joked.

His mouth slanted against mine over and over, and I was lost in the waves crashing against the beach while he peeled off his shirt, then followed it by removing mine. Clothes rustled, waves slammed the sand. The taste of wine blessed my tongue as he parted my lips again.

No more words were spoken.

They weren't needed.

Sometimes, the best conversations happened when you listened to the soft breaths of the person next to you, the sounds of nature around you, the air giving you life. And at the end of the day, the slow beats of someone's heart.

When it beat for you.

Chapter Thirteen

"All things end, but that also means all things begin, right?"—August Wellington

August

"More." I'd egged her on. I was desperate for more. I didn't even remember stripping us down as I thrust into her and rolled my hips, needing her more than anything in my life.

She didn't complain, just clung to me like she knew I needed the connection—as if she'd known the entire time, just like I did.

The fear.

The terror of finding a person you knew you could be with. A person you could also lose.

It was over almost before it began, and then, an hour later, she was on top of me again, moving her hips this time, gripping me by the hair and kissing down my chest. "Mmmmm, need more."

I met her movements. "I don't think I want to stop."

"Then don't."

So, we didn't.

Something beautiful was happening, something strange, something I was afraid to say out loud.

And the next day, when we both woke up to text messages from our families, it was an actual disaster.

Are you alive? Dad texted. *You left the tile from your keys at the campsite, huge storm.*

Hazel jolted awake and looked over at me. "Is your phone going off like crazy?"

"Shit." I scrambled naked out of bed, but my legs got tangled in the sheets. "I mean, it's not like we aren't consenting adults. Everything is fine, totally fine."

"Yeah." Her eyes roamed down my body. "So fine."

The sheet fell from her chest.

I gulped and tossed my phone. "They can wait, right?"

"Oh, please let them wait."

"I needed you," I admitted. "Mom's dying, and that's the worst lean-in as far as a conversation starter for more sex, but I've just been so—"

"August,"—she pressed a finger to my mouth—"I'll take this to my deathbed. But I know you. You can't just take it all on and hope that because you're strong it makes her body less weak."

Tears welled in my eyes. "I feel so damn selfish for wanting something for myself."

"What is it you want?" She pulled me under the sheet and wrapped her body around me. "Maybe I can give it to you."

Another tear slid down my cheek. "I think you already did, Hazel."

"My virginity?" she deadpanned.

I froze. "What!?"

She burst out laughing. "Oh my gosh, you should see your face."

"One." I started counting. "Two."

She scrambled out of bed and ran naked toward the shower. I joined her immediately and pushed her against the tile, kissing her senseless before pulling away.

Her hands gripped my biceps, pieces of blond hair sticking to her wet cheeks. "I really like you, August, you know, despite how argumentative you are. And weird. And how everything is just a big deal. I mean, who cares if it was a hole?"

I grinned. "Keep going."

"I know." She looked down. "I know you're going through a lot. Your mom's sick, and I know you've been taking on so much. I'm sorry I never said anything. I just didn't want it to be weird, so I figured a distraction was the best way. Immature?"

"Hazardous, but no." I laughed. "I needed a distraction. I don't think I've ever been so thankful to see my enemy graduate and throw a party."

Hazel took a deep breath. "I had a crush on you and thought you hated me."

"I had a crush on *you* and thought the only way to get your attention was to be annoying."

"Stupid, immature boys."

"Stupid, beautiful girls who climb trees."

I kissed her again when a knock sounded at the door.

We ignored it.

The knocking got louder, and voices were heard.

Finally, I grabbed a towel and wrapped it around my hips, then went to the door and jerked it open. "What the hell is so important that—oh shit. Hi, Mr. Titus. I was just, um…"

"Who is it?" Hazel ran around the corner in a towel and gaped. "Oh. Hi, Daddy, we were just…cleaning."

My dad stood behind him, arms crossed, then shook his head and whispered, "Told you they just needed some time together. Classic Nadine. Put them in a tough spot and… look, now we have grandkids."

Hazel gasped. "That is…certainly not—"

"Happening." Was I passing out? I had tunnel vision, then gripped her. "I mean, we're obviously dating now, but it wasn't because of you. It's not like you can control nature."

Mr. Titus handed over a crisp one-hundred-dollar bill to my dad and continued shaking his head. "I think I need a beer. I hate being wrong," Hazel's dad said.

"My wife called it," Dad replied. "She and Grandma bet three days before Grandma's passing."

"I'm sorry, what?" Hazel asked. "Bet what?"

Mr. Titus looked over his shoulder at Hazel. "I can't really make eye contact with you right now, but part of her will, and part of her bet with this one's mom"—he pointed at me—"was that when things got tense between you, all we needed to do was send you on a trip. Force you together. Grandma Nadine was convinced that you guys were in love, and so was your mom." Mr. Titus nodded his chin at me. "I mean, I still might kill you later, and for the love of God, put on some clothes, but it looks like I was wrong in this scenario. Grandma's matchmaking magic lives on. After all, she did matchmake almost everyone in this family." He shared a look with my dad. "Friends included."

Dad smiled. "Wouldn't change a thing. Now, let's go have that beer while we give them some privacy."

Both dads still looked like they wanted to ground us like we were twelve.

Instead, they walked off.

I closed the door.

It clicked shut.

Hazel stood still next to me. "They set us up."

"I can't decide if it's weird or if I should profusely thank them, which makes it even weirder."

Hazel dropped her towel. "Maybe we just focus on the present and go from there? Fill in some of those damaged emotional cracks, date, and get crazy. After all, Great-Grandma's never wrong."

I thought about my dad, about his marriage with my mom, about the good times despite the sadness, and I knew she was right. Maybe I wouldn't have a lot more time with my mom, but the moments she was given, wow…how spectacular.

"You're right." I pulled Hazel into my arms. "We all have our spiritual gifts. Hers was matchmaking."

"And mine?" Hazel asked.

"Digging holes."

"And yours?" She laughed.

"Standing by your side," I whispered. "For as long as you'll let me."

Chapter Fourteen

Hazel

ONE YEAR LATER

Dear Hazel,

If you're reading this, then that means I'm currently driving God to drink. Then again, water into wine, am I right? Anyway, I wanted to send you one last thing, and while I'm sitting here in this boring-as-hell room wondering when I'm gonna kick the bucket—high heels on, thank you very much—I figured I'd impart some wisdom on you.

The colors aren't black and white. Sometimes, they're gray. Other times, they're red, pink, blue, or yellow, just like one scar never looks the same as another. The way the love around you fills, it shifts and changes. It grows.

You'll have setbacks, you'll have some of the best days of your life, followed by days where you want to crawl into the corner or scream into a pillow. Humans are like earthquakes waiting to happen. You know there could be damage, but you keep going, you keep fighting. And then if or when it does happen, you manage it, you fix it. You allow the cracks to fill, and you keep going, knowing it could happen again. But you become wiser for it.

Marriage is like that, Hazel. Wear lipstick for you, not just for him. Dress up at least once a week, even if it means you're walking around your house by yourself. The three Ss never cease to solve all problems: a good shave, a shower, and sex—in whatever order you prefer. And at the end of the day, Hazel, my dear girl, if you're a mess, if you're chaos, if you're dirty, if you can't even look at yourself in the mirror and feel nothing but pain? Well done. You've lived.

What a wonderful gift. And tell that boy next door I'm sure you're about to marry that I knew it the minute he saw you in the tree reading your book. I knew it the second he smiled up at you like a puzzle he couldn't figure out but wanted to try, day in and day out, until all the pieces fit.

I hope you enjoy your time with that young man and give us so many grandchildren and great-grandchildren. If you look at the third branch on the right, where you used to stash wine—shhhh, I won't tell—you'll find a blue hairpin inside the little hole. You'll also find a picture of us. Do me a favor? Have your daddy carry that picture with him down the aisle. On our deathbeds, we think about a lot of crazy things. On mine, I just wanted to hold your hand and walk you toward your beginning before I met my end.

I love you, sweet pea.
Great-Grandma Nadine.

Epilogue

The Wedding

I held the picture in one hand and my dad's arm in the other, looking straight ahead. I stared at August waiting at the end of the aisle.

And in his hands, he held a picture of his mom and him.

Both of us, both of our losses, both of our broken pieces, were getting put back together, through us and our love. But also through two incredible women in our lives who actually saw it.

They didn't look up at the sky and claim it was falling.

They looked up in amazement and said, "Wow, how beautiful."

Even in the darkness and the chaos, they saw the one small part that made the world worth saving, worth living in, worth loving.

I walked with my dad and felt like sprinting toward August. We'd had a rough start, a weird middle, and so much laughter that it made my stomach hurt.

We'd have hard times.

We'd have good times.

We'd have disasters.

Wins.

And we'd have each other.

Being with someone who challenged you, who made you question, who made you wonder if it was worth the risk—it was a hazard.

But in the end, love truly did fix it all in the most beautifully messy way.

I didn't remember a lot of the ceremony until I handed the picture over to my dad and wrapped my arms around August. "Wanna fight?"

He burst out laughing. "Hazel, I've been fighting you since the minute I tried to push you out of that tree."

"I thought you were trying to save me."

"Nah, I was saving myself. Figured if I struck first, I wouldn't fall first."

"And did you?" I asked. "Fall first?"

"First." He kissed me. "Last." He kissed me again. "Forever."

"Forever." I grinned against his mouth.

THE END

* * * *

Also from 1001 Dark Nights and Rachel Van Dyken, discover Darkest Need, Mafia King, Provoke, Abandon, All Stars Fall, Envy, and The Anti-Fan and the Idol.

Sign up for the 1001 Dark Nights Newsletter
and be entered to win a Tiffany Key necklace.

There's a contest every month!

Go to www.1001DarkNights.com to subscribe.

**As a bonus, all subscribers can download
FIVE FREE exclusive books!**

Discover 1001 Dark Nights Collection Eleven

DRAGON KISS by Donna Grant
A Dragon Kings Novella

THE WILD CARD by Dylan Allen
A Rivers Wilde Novella

ROCK CHICK REMATCH by Kristen Ashley
A Rock Chick Novella

JUST ONE SUMMER by Carly Phillips
A Dirty Dare Series Novella

HAPPILY EVER MAYBE by Carrie Ann Ryan
A Montgomery Ink Legacy Novella

BLUE MOON by Skye Warren
A Cirque des Moroirs Novella

A VAMPIRE'S MATE by Rebecca Zanetti
A Dark Protectors/Rebels Novella

LOVE HAZARD by Rachel Van Dyken

BRODIE by Aurora Rose Reynolds
An Until Her Novella

THE BODYGUARD AND THE BOMBSHELL by Lexi Blake
A Masters and Mercenaries: New Recruits Novella

THE SUBSTITUTE by Kristen Proby
A Single in Seattle Novella

CRAVED BY YOU by J. Kenner
A Stark Security Novella

GRAVEYARD DOG by Darynda Jones
A Charley Davidson Novella

A CHRISTMAS AUCTION by Audrey Carlan
A Marriage Auction Novella

THE GHOST OF A CHANCE by Heather Graham
A Krewe of Hunters Novella

Also from Blue Box Press

LEGACY OF TEMPTATION by Larissa Ione
A Demonica Birthright Novel

VISIONS OF FLESH AND BLOOD by Jennifer L. Armentrout and Ravyn Salvador
A Blood & Ash and Fire & Flesh Compendium

FORGETTING TO REMEMBER by M.J. Rose

TOUCH ME by J. Kenner
A Stark International Novella

BORN OF BLOOD AND ASH by Jennifer L. Armentrout
A Flesh and Fire Novel

MY ROYAL SHOWMANCE by Lexi Blake
A Park Avenue Promise Novel

SAPPHIRE DAWN by Christopher Rice writing as C. Travis Rice
A Sapphire Cove Novel

EMBRACING THE CHANGE by Kristen Ashley
A River Rain Novel

IN THE AIR TONIGHT by Marie Force

LEGACY OF CHAOS by Larissa Ione
A Demonica Birthright Novel

Discover More Rachel Van Dyken

Darkest Need: A Dark Ones Novella

I see everything. I feel everything.

I watch people fall in love. I watch them burn with hate, anger, rage, and I see the cycle repeat over and over again. I take it on every night I work at Timber, aka Anubis's bar in downtown Seattle, and then I help the rest of the immortals keep the very intense balance between Heaven and Earth.

I see everyone's future but mine, and when I try to look, all I see is darkness, despair, need…

Until *she* walks into my bar with bruises on her face, getting pulled by one of the lesser demons. I do what any good bartender would do… I beat him within an inch of his life and turn my eyes to her.

By then, it's too late.

She already has me in her grasp.

A succubus that has no other plan than to suck me clean of every inch of power that's been bestowed on me by the Heavens.

I never thought my future involved getting kidnapped and tied up or that I'd die by way of sex—then again, maybe that's for the best. Dying at the hands of my enemy rather than being one more burden to my already mated friends.

After all, giving into one last need before death, while selfish, may be exactly what my darkness means.

My need is great.

And she's about to find out just how much.

* * * *

Mafia King: A Mafia Royals Novella

One of the first rules they give you when you're undercover—never fall for the enemy.

I didn't just fall for the enemy.

I became what I was supposed to hate.

What's worse: I fell in love with one.

I live a double life, and both sides know it's only a matter of time before I'm forced to choose.

Rebirth through mafia blood.

Or death at the hands of the very government I swore to protect.

I have one more job before my time's up.

I just wish it was anything but babysitting a mafia princess who's half my size but knows how to pack such a brutal punch I worry about my ability to have children.

Tin's small but terrifying.

And I'm her new bodyguard while we all go on a much-needed vacation.

I just have to stick to the plan.

And remember rule number one.

And stop kissing her.

* * * *

Provoke: A Seaside Pictures Novella

The music industry called me a savant at age sixteen when I uploaded my first video and gained instant fame. And then Drew Amherst of Adrenaline became my mentor, and my career took off.

Everything was great.

Until tragedy struck, and I wondered if I'd ever be able to perform again. I fought back, but all it took was a falling light to bring it all back to the fore. So, I walked away. Because I knew it wasn't just stage fright. It was so much more.

The only problem?

Drew and the guys are counting on me. If I can't combat the crippling anxiety threatening to kill me, I might lose more than I ever dreamed of.

Enter Piper Rayne, life coach, with her bullshit about empowerment, rainbows, and butterflies. She smiles all the damn time, and I'm ninety-nine percent sure there's not a problem she can't solve.

Until me.

She was given twenty-one days to fix me. To make me see what's important. What's real. The problem is, all I can see now is her. The sexy woman who pushes me. Provokes me.

Only time will tell if she's able to do her job—and I can make her mine.

* * * *

Abandon: A Seaside Pictures Novella

It's not every day you're slapped on stage by two different women you've been dating for the last year.

I know what you're thinking. What sort of ballsy woman gets on stage and slaps a rockstar? Does nobody have self-control anymore? It may have been the talk of the Grammys.

Oh, yeah, forgot to mention that. I, Ty Cuban, was taken down by two psychotic women in front of the entire world. Lucky for us the audience thought it was part of the breakup song my band and I had just finished performing. I was thirty-three, hardly ready to settle down.

Except now it's getting forced on me. Seaside, Oregon. My bandmates were more than happy to settle down, dig their roots into the sand, and start popping out kids. Meanwhile I was still enjoying life.

Until now. Until my forced hiatus teaching freaking guitar lessons at the local studio for the next two months. Part of my punishment, do something for the community while I think deep thoughts about all my life choices.

Sixty days of hell.

It doesn't help that the other volunteer is a past flame that literally looks at me as if I've sold my soul to the devil. She has the voice of an angel and looks to kill—I would know, because she looks ready to kill me every second of every day. I broke her heart when we were on tour together a decade ago.

I'm ready to put the past behind us. She's ready to run me over with her car then stand on top of it and strum her guitar with glee.

Sixty days. I can do anything for sixty days. Including making the sexy Von Abigail fall for me all over again. This time for good.

Damn, maybe there's something in the water.

* * * *

All Stars Fall: A Seaside Pictures/Big Sky Novella

She *left*.
Two words I can't really get out of my head.
She left *us*.
Three more words that make it that much worse.

Three being another word I can't seem to wrap my mind around.

Three kids under the age of six, and she left because she missed it. Because her dream had never been to have a family, no, her dream had been to marry a rockstar and live the high life.

Moving my recording studio to Seaside Oregon seems like the best idea in the world right now especially since Seaside Oregon has turned into the place for celebrities to stay and raise families in between touring and producing. It would be lucrative to make the move, but I'm doing it for my kids because they need normal, they deserve normal. And me? Well, I just need a break and help, that too. I need a sitter and fast. Someone who won't flip me off when I ask them to sign an Iron Clad NDA, someone who won't sell our pictures to the press, and most of all? Someone who looks absolutely nothing like my ex-wife.

He's tall.

That was my first instinct when I saw the notorious Trevor Wood, drummer for the rock band Adrenaline, in the local coffee shop. He ordered a tall black coffee which made me smirk, and five minutes later I somehow agreed to interview for a nanny position. I couldn't help it; the smaller one had gum stuck in her hair while the eldest was standing on his feet and asking where babies came from. He looked so pathetic, so damn sexy and pathetic that rather than be star-struck, I took pity. I knew though; I knew the minute I signed that NDA, the minute our fingers brushed and my body became insanely aware of how close he was—I was in dangerous territory, I just didn't know how dangerous until it was too late. Until I fell for the star and realized that no matter how high they are in the sky—they're still human and fall just as hard.

* * * *

Envy: An Eagle Elite Novella

Every family has rules, the mafia just has more....
Do not speak to the bosses unless spoken to.
Do not make eye contact unless you want to die.
And above all else, do not fall in love.
Renee Cassani's future is set.
Her betrothal is set.
Her life, after nannying for the five families for the summer, is set.
Somebody should have told Vic Colezan that.

He's a man who doesn't take no for an answer.
And he only wants one thing.
Her.
Somebody should have told Renee that her bodyguard needed as much discipline as the kids she was nannying.
Good thing Vic has a firm hand.

* * * *

The Anti-Fan and the Idol: A My Summer In Seoul Novella

Make it or break it...

Or maybe just break them?

Ai-Ri has been training under YK Management in Korea for two years without any results. She doesn't fit the typical mold for a successful K-POP idol image, literally down to her blood type. She has six more months before college entrance exams which means she only has six months to make it as an idol before her dreams are crushed.
Things take a turn when two of the most famous male idols break away from their group and decide to form their own co-ed group, a rarity.
And wonder of all wonders, they need one more girl.
It would be the perfect opportunity, except she hates them.
They are arrogant, entitled, rich little snobs who want the world to worship the ground they walk on. To make matters worse, the only reason they came to her was because they are desperate, which means she needs to prove herself even more.
Tempers and personalities collide when she's forced to either accept the position or give up on her dream.
But what happens when you suddenly go from anti-fan and enemy number one to stuck in a love triangle between two boys you were born to hate but are somehow falling in love with? And will the group survive the heartbreak that follows when she finally makes her choice?

Coming Soon!
Fallen Gods, Book 1
By Rachel Van Dyken
Coming December 4, 2024

Spellbinding new fantasy from #1 *New York Times* bestselling author Rachel Van Dyken…

* * * *

"Old myths, old gods, old heroes have never died. They are only sleeping at the bottom of our mind, waiting for our call. We have need for them. They represent the wisdom of our race."— Stanley Kunitz

"Did she accept?" My voice clips into the phone. I tap my foot and stare out at the cliff overlooking the sea.

"Yes, sir," Ingrid, my secretary says quickly, she's anxious with her words, like she knows what's happening next, but none of us, not even I, can prevent it. Fate is a cruel mistress and we're a constant slave . "She leaves in the next twenty-four hours."

"First class," I say, my voice lacking emotion, because when has that ever helped me? "Put her in the West Tower."

She makes a familiar noise in the back of her throat signaling that she's about to argue with me—sometimes it feels like she's more mother than secretary with her tight blond braid that I swear just continues to cause more wrinkles around her green eyes. "Are you sure that's a good idea—"

"Are you sure you'll stay employed if you finish that thought?" I snap.

"Sorry, sir." She sounds anything but sorry—I know her thoughts on this, I always have, but we all have our parts to play and she often times, more recently, needs to be reminded of hers. It's tiring, this life.

But balance will always outweigh chaos.

And power will always overcome death.

I drop the call without saying goodbye; there's no need. She knows better, and she knows how this works. I stare out over the sea. The wind picks up outside as waves crash against the rocks. The swells grow higher and higher. The sea groans in anticipation, the water will be like this for a while.

History, will always repeat itself. How tragic. How necessary.

It's almost comical how angry the water suddenly gets when it senses yet another shift in the universe. Time never truly stands still; it's continuous in its wrath, always moving, never pausing, shifting from one thing to another.

By the time I'm outside, the weather's gone from sunny to angry, like it can sense what's about to happen or maybe it's pissed about what's been happening, what needs to continue to happen in order to keep those waves where they belong—in the fjord.

"Settle down, Ken," I murmur, knowing he can hear the vibrations of my voice through the wind, even if he doesn't want to. A giant crack sounds in the distance as a tree snaps in half on the small island, hurling itself into the water. Nature's throwing a small tantrum as per usual.

I snort out a laugh of amusement, so testy. "Yeah, well fuck you too."

I turn my back on the crashing waves, close my eyes, and breathe in the salty breeze. I start walking but stop at the large oak tree in the middle of the back property and press my hand to it, then lean my body against it until my forehead touches the warm rough bark. Strength flows through me, renews my body. I swear I can see the deepness of the three large roots below my feet feeding off the earth, giving life, taking it.

"It wasn't always like this, was it?" I say mostly to myself. "It's almost like I can't remember anymore."

Or maybe it's that I really don't want to. Because who truly would?

Only a monster.

The wind suddenly dies down and I go back into my house to tell my staff to prepare yet again for its next guest.

And get to work.

About Rachel Van Dyken

Rachel Van Dyken is the #1 New York Times, Wall Street Journal, and USA Today bestselling author of over 90 books ranging from contemporary romance to paranormal. With over four million copies sold, she's been featured in Forbes, US Weekly, and USA Today. Her books have been translated in more than 15 countries. She was one of the first romance authors to have a Kindle in Motion book through Amazon publishing and continues to strive to be on the cutting edge of the reader experience. She keeps her home in the Pacific Northwest with her husband, adorable sons, naked cat, and lazy dog.

You can connect with her on Facebook:
www.facebook.com/rachelvandyken
or join her fan group Rachel's New Rockin Readers:
https://www.facebook.com/groups/RRRFanClub.

For more information, visit her website at:
http://rachelvandykenauthor.com

On Behalf of 1001 Dark Nights,
Liz Berry, M.J. Rose, and Jillian Stein would like to thank ~

Steve Berry
Doug Scofield
Benjamin Stein
Kim Guidroz
Chelle Olson
Tanaka Kangara
Asha Hossain
Chris Graham
Jessica Saunders
Stacey Tardif
Dylan Stockton
Kate Boggs
Richard Blake
and Simon Lipskar

Made in the USA
Middletown, DE
06 May 2024